Texas Ranger Jeb Powers:

Jeb's Quest

by Judy Goodspeed

Western Novel from
Dragonfly Publishing, Inc.

JEB'S QUEST

Western Novel
Released in 2021

Paperback Edition
EAN 978-1-949187-36-6
ISBN 1-949187-36-5

Published in the United States of America by
Dragonfly Publishing, Inc.
Website: www.dragonflypubs.com

TABLE OF CONTENTS

Dedication

To my great-great nieces, Brooklyn King and Rosie Ford, two special little girls who meet challenges every day and deal with them bravely.

Acknowledgements

Thank you, Johnnie Wingo, for your knowledge of westerns and your love of reading. You are deeply appreciated along with members of Writing For Fun — Paula, David, Betty, Debbie, Nora, Jaydyn, and Glenda.

Thank you also to Evelyn Wootten, Mary Zilm, and Paula Moradi for reading my manuscript and making suggestions.

Thanks Terri Branson, publisher of Dragonfly, for believing in me and putting up with my poor computer skills. You're the best.

Creek Words

Chabon
(Boy) *Cepvne*

Fooswah
(Bird) *Fuswv*

Hoktee
(Girl) *Hoktee*

Mado
(Thank You) *Mvto*

Osekee
(Rain) *Oske*

Thlopthlocco
(Tall Cane or Big Reed)

Part I

Jebediah

CHAPTER 1

RAIN, cold and relentless beat down, but Jeb Powers stayed motionless, as though molded into the tree trunk he leaned against.

Icy raindrops dripped from his flat-brimmed black hat, trickled under his oilskin raincoat collar, and then ran down his back. There was no wind, no sun, just the continuous patter of rain combined with the sound of rushing water in the North Canadian River.

He yearned to mount his horse and leave this miserable country. Yet duty compelled him to stay, and to move meant an almost certain death. It was times like these when he questioned his decision to become a Texas Ranger. Then he thought of the man Henry Burris had killed for two dollars and the young girl he had kidnapped, raped, and murdered.

Despite the possibility he might be found frozen to that tree trunk, Jeb was determined to stay put until Burris made his move.

Bare-limbed trees were the only protection Burris had, so he'd have to do something soon. With Jeb hot on his trail, he had lost his pack, his horse was lame, and his canteen was empty. He was trapped on the north by the river and on the west by a creek running brim-full. To the east was a maze of briars and undergrowth. To the south waited a lawman that wouldn't hesitate to shoot. Added to his dilemma was the fact he had no slicker, while clouds building in the north meant snow or sleet was headed toward them.

With each passing minute, the clouds drew closer, and the already cold air grew even colder. Jeb knew he could wait out Burris, but the need for a cup of coffee gave him an idea.

"Hey Burris!" he called. "Come on out, and I'll brew us a pot of coffee. Might even fry the rabbit I caught yesterday."

"Good try," the outlaw answered. "How do you plan to build a fire?"

"Got some wood covered with a canvas. Just pitch out your gun and mosey on over."

"You know I ain't going back to Texas."

"Can't say as I blame you. I don't reckon you'd get a cordial greeting. What say I just take you to Fort Smith?"

"I have your word on that?"

"Yep."

When Jeb heard the outlaw begin to move, he slipped behind the tree.

Sure enough a shot rang out, and a bullet slammed into the trunk. Then Burris rushed from his hiding place.

"You missed," Jeb said. "Drop your gun, or I'll save myself a trip to Arkansas."

Burris dropped his pistol. "Damn."

"Come on over with your hands on top of your head."

Burris shuffled into view. He was a terrible mess with tattered clothes, a scraggy black beard, and long hair hanging from under his floppy hat.

Jeb didn't waste any time handcuffing him and patting him down for a hidden weapon.

Once satisfied, he sat the prisoner under a cottonwood and whistled for Tulip. The little burro came trotting out of the trees, made a wide circle around the cottonwood, and then stood beside her master. Jeb had found Tulip as a baby in a burned-out homestead near the Mexican border. He had raised her on goat's milk, and they had been together since.

Although she was wet, he gave her a pat. "Keep an eye on him."

She planted herself in front of Burris.

"I ain't scared of no jackass," Burris said and started to stand.

Tulip gave him a not-so-gentle butt with her head and down he went.

"She don't cotton to being called a jackass," Jeb informed.

The rain stopped, but from the looks of the sky it was going to start snowing or sleeting any minute. Feeling a sudden drop in temperature, Jeb shivered. It must have dropped ten degrees. He uncovered his stash of wood and used one of his carefully hoarded lucifers to start a fire. He was poorly equipped for freezing weather, but some hot coffee and food would help. It didn't take long to put on the coffeepot, and then cut up the rabbit and put it into the skillet. While it fried, he rummaged through Burris' pack, took out a coat, and draped it around the outlaw's shoulders.

Hot coffee and fried rabbit lifted his spirits, but he had a battle in front of him. It was bad enough having to deal with the killer, but early March in Oklahoma Indian Territory might be his undoing. He stood with his rear to the fire, sipped coffee, and tried to dry out the seat of his trousers. Riding in wet drawers made for a galled butt, and he was uncomfortable enough without that. The fact that he had no idea where they were added to his discomfort.

While Burris finished off the rabbit, Jeb gathered his horse, Brownie, tied the pack onto Tulip, and caught the outlaw's lame horse.

"Get up," Jeb ordered.

"I don't feel much like riding in this weather," Burris said.

"You ain't riding. You're walking. Now on your feet, or I'll tie you to my saddle horn and drag you."

"My horse ain't hurt bad. I can ride him."

"No, you can't. About three steps and he'll be lame for sure. Now shut your mouth, get on your feet, and head south."

When the sleet hit, Jeb was thankful to have the wind at his back. He couldn't remember ever having been this cold. Before they had traveled a mile, both men and animals were covered with ice. Tree limbs drooped from the extra weight, and frozen grass crunched beneath hooves.

If he didn't find cover soon, there would be no need to worry about Fort Smith.

Burris stumbled, fell, and didn't get up.

Jeb struggled to get unstuck from the saddle. When he finally got off his horse, he slipped and fell.

Seizing his chance, Burris jumped to his feet and ran. Tulip caught him and knocked him down. He got up, and she knocked him down again.

As Jeb seriously considered shooting Burris, he spotted smoke just up ahead. The thought of shelter and a fire perked him up enough to string a rope around the outlaw and remount. He wanted to hurry, but couldn't expect a man on foot to keep up, so he reined in his horse.

The way the smoke moved made it hard to pin down its origin. Jeb couldn't feel his hands or feet. They had quit hurting some time back, so he feared they were frostbitten.

"I can't go no further," Burris called.

That's when the cabin came into sight, and Jeb knew the smoke was real. The structure wasn't much, but the stack of wood on the porch was impressive.

"Stay put," Jeb said to Burris.

"Don't be long, or I'll be froze to death."

Jeb reached to get his badge out of his shirt pocket, but couldn't feel it. He fumbled around until it fell out into the snow. He used both hands to scoop it up.

"Hello the house!" he hollered, instead of knocking on the door.

The door opened a crack to reveal a small elderly woman. She looked at the badge he held up, but did not seem to understand it. After a moment, she opened the door for him.

Once inside, Jeb almost fainted from relief. He tried to explain they needed to warm by the fire and care for the animals. He didn't know how long he jabbered before he realized she didn't understand a word he was saying. Using sign language, he managed to make her understand. When she nodded, he thought he might survive after all.

He brought Burris into the kitchen and sat him in the corner. Jeb doubted the man would be any trouble, but tied his feet and checked the handcuffs. The pack on Tulip was covered with ice. Jeb hated to take it into the cabin, but did it anyway for fear of losing what little food he had left. Then he took the burro and horses to the lean-to, scraped as much ice off them as possible, and fed them each a little corn from his dwindling supply. He'd worry about water later.

Before he reached the cabin, Jeb's teeth began to chatter and chills ripped through his body. Once inside the change in temperature threw him into shock. Before he could make it to a chair, he slid down the wall and sat on the plank floor. When heat began to penetrate his fingers and toes, the pain was almost unbearable. He gritted his teeth and whimpered, while Burris hollered and cussed.

The woman held a quilt in front of the fireplace for a moment and then wrapped it around Jeb. When the chills lessened, she spooned warm broth into his mouth.

Long minutes passed, but finally the pain subsided and exhaustion took its place.

* * * * *

CHAPTER 2

COLD crept into the cabin, rousing Jeb from deep sleep.

He shivered, drew the quilt tighter around himself, and struggled to sit. Why was his head hurting and why had the fire gone out in the hearth?

He grasped the doorframe and pulled himself to his feet. The room swam in a dizzy circle, and there was two of everything. When his eyes began to focus, he checked on Burris. The outlaw was gone.

How could he have gotten away without waking him, or the woman warning him? Where was she?

He leaned against the wall and took stock of his surroundings. Burris was gone, the pack was gone, handcuffs lay discarded on the floor, and the woman sat tied to a chair in the far corner of the room.

Jeb wobbled to her, took the gag from her mouth, and untied her. She started talking and gesturing rapidly. From the scene she created, he understood that Burris hit him in the head with a stick of firewood, tied her up, grabbed the pack, and left. Well, he certainly had a headache, and after a little searching found a large lump but no blood. He was surprised the outlaw didn't kill him. Maybe Burris thought he had.

He stirred the coals and added wood to the fireplace. The wood caught quickly, which meant Burris hadn't been gone long enough for the coals to die. After breaking the film of ice on the water bucket, Jeb filled the coffee pot. The woman busied about, stirring together something in a big bowl. Once mixed to her satisfaction, she poured it in a pot and hung the pot on a hook over the fireplace.

While the coffee water boiled, Jeb checked on the animals. Sometime in the night sleet had changed to snow. Ice covered with snow was dangerous for travel. Burris' lame horse and Tulip were in the lean-to, but Brownie was gone. He dreaded the thought of walking, but didn't have another option. Well, he was going to have coffee first and maybe a bowl of whatever the woman was cooking.

Jeb was shivering by the time he returned to the cabin. He was ill-equipped to go after Burris. It would be easy to forget about the outlaw and head south. Following that thought, Jeb recalled the Ranger Creed: *No man in the wrong can stand up to a man in the right who just keeps on a-comin'.*

Well, he would be coming alright, even if slowly.

Before he left, he carried in an armload of firewood. After entering the cabin, he stacked the wood near the fireplace. He then took the water bucket and axe to the creek. It didn't take long to break the ice and fill the bucket. Just a few minutes outside in the cold was enough to cause him to shake. Once back inside, he savored the warmth of the cabin. Jeb set the filled bucket on top of a tall and narrow wooden stand that already held a wash bowl.

The mush the woman gave him was not flavorful, but it was warm and filling. He ate two helpings, drank weak coffee, and then took in his surroundings. The one room cabin was small, snug, and very clean. A large fireplace took most of one wall with two rocking chairs sitting in front. A table and four straight back chairs sat just beyond the rocking chairs. The space below a couple of shelves, that were covered with a cloth curtain, served as storage for dishes. From one of those shelves, the woman took bowls and cups. Pegs and hooks along the walls contained clothing and a variety of objects crafted from beads and feathers. A bed took up most of the west wall. Jeb wanted to find out about the woman, but didn't have time. Burris already had a good start.

The sorry varmint took his pack, coat, gloves, rifle, and pistol. The dull pocket knife Jeb carried seemed a poor weapon. Maybe he could borrow the quilt. It would provide some warmth. Gesturing, he pulled it around him as if to ask if it was okay to take it. She shook her head and went to a trunk at the end of the bed. From it she took a heavy buffalo robe and something else.

She placed a gun in his hand. He looked it over. It was an old .45 loaded with two bullets. Two shots were better than none, he thought as he stuck the heavy pistol in his waistband. Then she handed him the robe. Jeb looked at her and shook his head. This was the first time he noticed she had bright blue eyes.

"I can't take this. You might need it."

"Aye," she said, motioning toward the door.

Jeb pointed to himself. "I'm Jeb."

"Jeb," she repeated and then pointed to herself. "Fooswah."

He tried to repeat after her, but made a bit of a mess of it.

Putting on the robe, he looked at her. "I'll be back."

She walked onto the porch with him and waited while he took Tulip from the lean-to.

"I'll leave some corn for the horse," he said, handing her the little that was left in a sack.

She nodded and stood on the porch, while the ranger and the burro walked away.

Jeb had no trouble following Burris' trail, but the ice made it slow. Jeb used Tulip to steady him and together they made pretty good time. At a couple of sloping areas, it looked like Brownie had slid a little but managed to keep his feet. The little burro didn't miss a step, even with Jeb holding onto her.

It was cloudy and cold with the promise of more snow. If it did snow, he would lose Burris' tracks, so he pushed a little harder. He didn't worry about being out in the open, because he figured the outlaw was trying to out-distance him.

Travel was harder when they entered a cluster of trees. Limbs cracked, popped like gunshots, and then dropped from the weight of the ice.

Jeb stopped to rest and listened for anything unusual. With caution he pushed forward.

It seemed like he had traveled ten miles, but five was more likely the real distance. The sky darkened, and a gust of wind from the north sent a chill through him. Snow was coming, and there was no cover except ice-laden trees. Thank goodness for the robe the woman had given him. Only his hands and feet were cold.

Deep in thought, he was startled when Tulip stepped in front of him at the edge of a deep gully. Both burro and man slipped and slid down the side, but stopped before landing in the freezing water.

When he came to a halt, Jeb was shocked to see Brownie down the creek a way. The horse stood with his head down, shivering. Burris was nowhere in sight.

Jeb surveyed the area. It appeared that Brownie had slipped and then struggled to his feet. Footprints indicated Burris had left the saddle as Brownie went down, perhaps in fear of getting trapped under the horse.

Brownie started to Jeb, limping on his right front leg. A close inspection revealed an ice-packed hoof. Each step caused pressure on the tender center of the hoof. Jeb chipped away the ice with his pocketknife, hoping the horse would be okay to ride. He was.

He checked Tulip's hooves and received a nip on the backside for his effort.

"No bread for you tonight," he told the little burro.

He picked up the trail in a short time and felt confident he would soon have cuffs on the outlaw. There was a small problem. Burris had his rifle.

Jeb had a worn-out pistol and two old bullets. The odds were better than they had been half an hour ago, but his optimism changed somewhat when snow began to cover Burris' tracks. If he changed direction, Jeb would never find him.

The snow stopped, and clouds drifted apart to reveal blue sky. A break in the weather might help his luck some. Couldn't hurt it any. Just when he thought his situation had improved, the sun shone brightly on the snow-covered ground.

Jeb squinted and held his hand over his eyes, but still could hardly see. He tugged his hat brim down on his forehead and continued onward.

"This ain't gonna do," he told Brownie. "My head is about to bust from the sun glare. Think I'll forget the outlaw and go home."

A gunshot echoed through the frigid air.

Jeb headed southeast, the direction of the sound. The snow, ice, and blinding sunlight held him to a crawl, and rushing onto the scene might be suicide. He rode cautiously, taking in his surroundings, knowing Burris might have set a trap hoping to lure him within rifle range.

Every few minutes, Jeb reined in Brownie and sat listening to the stillness. Nothing moved.

* * * * *

CHAPTER 3

TEN, perhaps fifteen minutes later, Brownie snorted and shied away from something near a large pecan tree. Jeb drew his pistol.

He knew it wasn't Burris, or he would already be carrying a bullet. He rode to the tree and found a dead Indian boy beneath the drooping limbs. A careful inspection told an interesting story.

There were several hoof prints around, one set of boot prints, and a dead youth. Burris had shot the boy for his horse, but who were the other riders?

Tulip brayed.

In the blink of an eye Jeb was surrounded by a group of young braves. Before he could make them understand that he was friendly, they began beating on him. A sharp blow to the head knocked him out.

When he came to, he found himself belly-down across the saddle with his feet and hands tied together underneath Brownie's belly.

The riders were Indians, but he wasn't sure what tribe. Hanging upside down on a horse didn't allow him to observe much except the ground. Jeb lifted his head once in a while, but the strain was too much. Soon he gave up trying to figure out where they were going.

Finally, one of the men cut the rawhide that bound Jeb, jerked him from the saddle, and pushed him up a set of steps into what looked like a trading post.

A large man with fiery red hair stepped from behind a wood counter. "Why did you kill my son?" he asked, and then turned to a tall Indian. "Get a rope."

"I didn't kill your son," Jeb said. "Before you do any hanging, you'd better look in my pocket."

"Why would I look in your pocket? Money won't help you none." Grumbling, the man reached into Jeb's pocket and pulled out his badge. "This don't mean nothin' to me. You could have stole it for all I know."

"You're right. I could have, but I didn't. I was sent here after an outlaw named Henry Burris. Caught him at the Canadian, but he got away last night. I was on his trail when I heard a gunshot, so I headed in the direction of the sound. That's how I found the body."

"Maybe you're Henry Burris."

"My name's Jeb Powers. A lone woman in a cabin near the Canadian took us in last night. Her name is Foos something or other. She fed us and wound up tied in a chair. Burris knocked me out, took my weapons, and left on my horse. She gave me an old pistol and the buffalo robe."

"She gave you the robe? My son was wearing one when he left this morning."

"Burris probably took it along with your boy's horse."

"I know Fooswah," the red-haired man said, and then rattled off a bunch of Indian words to a couple of the men who had captured Jeb.

They left.

"I suppose they're going to check my story, and that's fine with me. While we wait, could I get something to eat? Pickin's have been pretty thin in this weather."

Again, the man rattled off something, and another man left the room. He returned with a bowl of stew and a chunk of bread.

"Thanks. I'm obliged." Jeb made quick work of the meal. "Something puzzled me when I found the boy. There were several hoof prints around the tree where he lay. Burris was on foot."

"I thought you said he took your horse."

"He did, but left him behind when he came up lame from an ice ball in his hoof. I dug it out, and he was fine to ride."

"Well, mister, you might be telling the truth. A couple of Indians were by here earlier. One of my hands speaks a little Comanche. He understood them to say they were looking for a man to go to Texas with them. Seems one of them just found out he has a son back there and plans to go get him. Said the man he was looking for was a breed that knew the Texas country well."

Jeb pondered that for a moment. "Sounds like Burris, but he sure didn't want me to take him to Texas. Maybe he'll go if he has some friends with him. Wonder how they knew he was in this country?"

"Don't think they said. I'm going to leave you untied, but don't plan on wandering off. My wife is going to go crazy when she hears about our son. When the men return and I know what you say is true, you'll be free to go. You're in the middle of Creek Indian territory. Even though they are more civilized than most tribes, they will kill if necessary."

"Can I get some supplies gathered up while I wait? I need food, grain, and a good rifle."

"Gather what you need. I'd go with you, if I could. I'm going to leave it to you to take care of Henry Burris, if my people don't find him first.

With snow falling, it will be hard hunting."

"I'll find him. You can count on it. What's your name? I'll let you know when he's hung or shot."

"Owen Hunter."

Jeb went through the shelves of goods, selecting beans, coffee, a slab of bacon, a tin of crackers, a few cans of peaches, some jerked beef, a rather worn coat, a couple of blankets, a split oilskin that would fit over the saddle, a knife, and a box of lucifers. He then grabbed a rifle and a pistol with enough ammunition for both. His biggest finds were a pair of gloves and a sack of shelled corn. Each item was listed on the back of an old wanted poster, tallied and signed.

Since Burris relieved Jeb of his money this was an IOU, but he would make it good.

* * * * *

CHAPTER 4

JEB checked on Tulip and Brownie. He found them snug and warm with corn in the feed trough.

He went to the creek, broke the ice, and dipped a bucketful. Both animals drank eagerly.

Returning from the shed, he noticed a group of riders approaching. One in the bunch caught his eye. After careful observation, he realized it was a her. Fooswah, whose name Jeb had learned meant Bird in Creek, rode with her chin up and back straight, as if born on a horse. A firm grip on the reins kept her mount under control.

Walking out to meet them, Jeb offered her a hand down, and she accepted. Once on the ground, she spoke to one of the braves.

"She wants to know if you are unharmed."

"Tell her I'm okay, thanks to the warm buffalo robe."

She nodded and went inside. That's when the wailing began. Jeb wanted to cover his ears. The pain of their loss gave him all the more reason to find Henry Burris.

The place filled with mourners, some arriving on horseback, others walking or in wagons. Jeb went to the shed to put the pack on Tulip and then saddle Brownie. He wanted away from the sadness and the senseless murder. Darkness closed in, but he still thought of leaving. Why did Burris shoot the boy? He could have easily taken his horse. It made no sense, but nothing about Burris made sense. He seemed to enjoy killing. Jeb puzzled over why the outlaw spared him. Maybe he just didn't want a passel of rangers after him. Well, he intended to give him misery enough for a dozen.

He walked through the falling snow back to the store. Once there, he left the robe and the pistol on the counter.

A young brave intercepted Jeb, as he walked to the shed. "No need go tonight."

"I need to keep up with them, or they'll outdistance me."

"They camp," the young brave said. "We go first light. You sleep."

Jeb piled up a bunch of straw, wrapped his new blanket around him, and laid his head on his saddle. If the braves knew where the outlaws were, it shouldn't be too hard to catch them.

Although dead tired, he couldn't sleep. His mind worried over the woman, who undoubtedly was a white captive. He would return after he dealt with Burris and, if possible, reunite Fooswah with her family. Something told him that wasn't going to be an easy task.

Blue eyes weren't that uncommon, but Fooswah's eyes sparkled like a cut diamond. Then it dawned on him. Bart Jamison's eyes were that same brilliant blue.

Jeb had run across Bart a few years ago, while chasing a couple of outlaws up near the Cimarron River in Indian Territory. Jamison had been trying to rescue a young girl held captive by a band of Comanches. In their time together, Jeb learned that Bart's aunt became a captive years before and his father had searched for her until his death. Could Fooswah be Bart's long-lost aunt? After either arresting or killing Burris, he would try to find Bart and tell him about the blue-eyed woman.

By midmorning, the trading post mourners began to arrive. The wake would last for days. A solemn column of mourners followed, as young men carried the boy's body to the Methodist Church in Thlopthlocco, the center of the Creek Nation.

Two braves rode up, as Jeb led Brownie and Tulip from the shed. He swung a leg over the saddle. Then he followed the two young men, heading west.

There was no falling weather, but the overcast sky kept the temperature below freezing. Jeb reminded himself the outlaws were also miserable.

They rode about three hours before one of the braves found a trail. Jeb hoped they would overtake the outlaws before dark, but that didn't happen. They made camp in a low place near a small frozen stream. Jeb fed the horses and Tulip a bait of corn, and broke the ice so they could drink. He would risk a small fire for a cup of coffee and some bacon.

Dawn came slowly, but it brought the promise of sunshine and warmth. Jeb's spirits rose a bit when he found a pile of horse manure with fresh steam rising from it. The outlaws were riding worn-out horses. By pushing hard, he thought they would find them in another hour or two.

A dead horse confirmed his suspicion. One of the braves spotted the carcass and alerted the others. They spread out and rode to the animal. One of the renegades had cut a hunk of meat from the horse's rump.

Jeb pushed harder. If they ate, it would be raw horsemeat, because he didn't intend to give them time to cook. He didn't see any boot tracks, so two were riding double. The tired horse wouldn't last long.

The day grew warmer, and ice fell from weary tree limbs. The warmth was welcome but not the showers of ice-cold water. Not a critter stirred or a bird chirped. The tracks of the horses and now the footprints of one man mapped their route on the white landscape. One of the men was walking to save the horses.

In the distance Jeb saw a small group of hills. From the direction of the tracks, they were headed for them. He motioned to the braves. They kicked into a lope, hoping to catch the three before they reached the foothills.

Just as they entered a stand of elm trees, one of the braves wheeled his horse and signaled for Jeb.

From the signs it was clear that Burris and his friends now had other friends. The disturbed ground indicated about five new riders had joined Burris and his pals. Jeb studied the tracks, until he found one unlike the others. The tracks of a pigeon-toed horse stood out like a black eye. As long as they stayed together, he could track them.

Three against eight seemed awfully lopsided, but that was the hand they were dealt. Indians were unpredictable. They might ride hard for two or three days, kill a buffalo or a deer, and feast for a couple of days. There remained the chance of them setting up an ambush or sending a brave or two to get behind Jeb. He must remain alert.

When the sun started to sink in the western sky, Jeb found a place to camp. A large hackberry tree with low hanging branches offered shelter and concealed the smoke from their campfire. While the braves searched for dry wood, Jeb unsaddled Brownie, took the pack off Tulip, and removed the packsaddle. The little burro stretched, shook, and walked around looking for a bite of something. Jeb fed her a handful of corn.

"Tulip," Jeb said, "guard the camp, while we get some shut-eye."

In the early morning, Tulip nudged Jeb.

He reached for his pistol, eased to his feet, and stood against a tree trunk. The two braves must have decided to go home. Jeb didn't blame them. He might do the same, if he had a home.

With that thought, he crawled back in his bedroll.

* * * * *

CHAPTER 5

JEB fried bacon and broke out the tin of crackers. Tulip trotted over and begged for one, which she got, of course.

He broke camp and picked up the trail of the Indians. He kept an even, unhurried pace with his rifle handy. The hilly country provided excellent places to meet a bullet. He tried to keep to low-lying areas and topped each rise carefully. Much to his relief, the sun shone bright and clear. Perhaps that meant no more snow and rain today.

Smoke caught his attention. He kicked Brownie into a lope and urged Tulip to follow. It was too much smoke for a campfire. Jeb pulled Brownie up to survey the situation. Maybe an ambush? With that thought, he decided to sneak around on foot. He tied Brownie with a slipknot, so he could get loose if Jeb didn't get back. Tulip could smell an Indian from a great distance, so he brought her along.

It took him some time to approach the source of the smoke. The frame of a burned-out wagon stood near a small stream. A man and woman lay dead, their heads scalped and bodies mangled. The sight took his breath.

Jeb circled the area and picked up the tracks of several horses. The large, wide hoof tracks of the wagon team were among them. He returned to Brownie and rode back to the wagon to bury the couple.

He found part of a shovel and began digging as best he could. Tulip nudged him and walked away. Jeb paused to look at his surroundings. Not noticing anything unusual, he continued digging.

Tulip came back and gave him another nudge. This time Jeb followed her to a growth of willows.

"I don't see a thing," Jeb scolded.

The burro nudged him again. Once more he parted the willows and this time looked into the eyes of a little boy.

"Hello," he said in a soft voice. "Are you hurt?"

The youngster shook his head.

"You stay here with Tulip. I'll be right back." Jeb removed his coat and draped it around the shivering child. "Tulip, stay with him."

With that command he reached in the pack and handed the little guy and the burro a couple of crackers.

Returning to Brownie, he pulled his ground cover sheet from behind the saddle and spread it over the bodies.

Jeb struggled with the poor excuse of a shovel. He worried about the boy, while he scooped out two shallow graves in the frozen ground. It was the best he could do with what he had. With respect he moved the bodies to their final resting place, covered them, and said a prayer.

He made a careful study of the burned-out wagon, looking for anything left behind that might be helpful. When nothing was found, he returned to the boy, wondering what to do with him.

One more time he surveyed the area around the wagon and campsite. From the tracks, there appeared to have been several horses. The torn-up ground didn't tell him much, until he spotted the print of a pigeon-toed hoof. Burris' tally sheet was getting longer. They were headed west, but that covered a lot of territory.

He needed to be gone from this place. With that thought, he returned to the little boy. When he parted the willows, he found the child curled up against Tulip and fast asleep.

Trying not to frighten him, Jeb gently laid his hand on the boy's shoulder.

The boy awoke with a start and jumped to his feet. Wild-eyed and terrified he turned to run, but Tulip blocked his path.

"It's okay son," Jeb said. "I'm not going to hurt you. You need to come with me, so we can get away from here. I know you're scared. So am I, but sitting still ain't going to help."

That said, Jeb held out his hand. After a bit of hesitation the boy took it. Jeb needed his coat, so he took it off the child, replaced it with a blanket, and then sat the boy in the saddle.

"Come on, Tulip," he said, as he mounted behind the boy.

He needed to find Burris, but his first task was taking care of this small person whose world had just been turned upside down.

The sun promised to disappear soon, so Jeb needed to find a good place to camp, risk a fire, and cook up a hot meal. He searched until he found a trail that held no tracks. The wet ground would make it hard to conceal his direction.

After several miles of riding, he spotted a large downed cottonwood tree with a scattering of trees around it. He lifted the boy from the saddle and sat him under the low hanging branches of the cottonwood where it was reasonably dry.

"I'm going to gather some firewood," he said.

Tulip stood nearby keeping an eye out for danger while Jeb searched for suitable wood. When he found enough for a fire, he reached inside his shirt to retrieve a bit of cotton to use as a starter. In no time, the fire was going. Although it didn't put out much warmth, it was comforting.

Jeb put the coffee pot on a rock near the fire, sliced bacon into the skillet, and fished some bread out of his pack.

Tulip appeared, nose in the air.

"You can't have any bread yet, you ornery varmint," Jeb told the burro. "We have a guest to share with, so be patient." As he worked, Jeb glanced at the boy. "My name's Jebediah Powers. Folks mostly call me Jeb. What's your name?"

"Russell McQueery, but folks mostly call me Russ."

Jeb stuck out his hand. "Mighty glad to meet you, Russ. You hungry?"

"Yes, sir."

"Well, come on and fill your plate. Do you drink coffee?"

"No, sir. Ma says I'm not old enough."

"How old are you?"

"I'm six, going on seven."

"Ma's usually know what's best, but a sip or two might warm you up some."

"I am pretty cold," was the reply.

Russ ate his bacon, but most of his biscuit went to a pesky burro. He drank a little coffee, but didn't seem to like it much.

It was going to be a cold night, so Jeb scattered some hot coals on the ground. Once they cooled, he moved them off. The ground under where they'd been was warm. He placed his bed roll on the spot and helped Russ remove his shoes.

"Climb in," he told the boy.

"Where are you going to sleep?" Russ asked.

"Right over here. Don't worry. I won't leave you. If you wake up, and I'm gone it's because I'm checking around so nobody sneaks up on us."

"Could Tulip stay with me?"

"You bet. Just call her over."

Russ didn't waste any time falling asleep with Tulip beside him.

Jeb sat a spell with his coffee and pondered his choices. It didn't make sense to continue after Burris with a child in tow. The best thing to do would be find a family somewhere and leave the boy with them, until he could find some of his kin. Russ must be his first concern. He would worry about Burris later. Jeb knew the direction the outlaws were headed. A delay in time shouldn't be a big problem, unless they went to Palo Duro, a maze of canyons that housed the Comanche. Any white men who ventured there were never seen again.

The little boy whimpered in his sleep, bringing Jeb's thoughts back to him and his family. What possessed a man to bring his wife and child into hostile country in the middle of a snowstorm? Even wagon trains were not completely safe, but made more sense than traveling alone. Maybe they hoped to get where they were going before the Indians came out of their winter camps. Russ might know where his parents had been headed, but Jeb should wait for the information to be volunteered. Firing a bunch of questions would not help the situation.

If he took Russ straight to Fort Sill, they would be riding through the middle of Apache, Comanche, and Kiowa territory. Any one of these tribes would take a scalp in the blink of an eye. The best way to cross that region was to go fast and stay as hidden as possible. That would be hard to do with a child and a burro.

Jeb began to drift off. Jerking awake, he sat up straight in his blankets.

He would take Russ to Fooswah. She would understand his plight better than anyone.

* * * * *

CHAPTER 6

ONCE again, Jeb tried to relax.

Before sleep came, it occurred to him that Russ would be terrified of staying with Indians, even though these were good Indians. He needed to explain what he had in mind.

This reminded him of his own childhood, how alone he had felt when his parents and sister died of cholera. He sat with their bodies for two days before a neighbor found him. Good old Homer took four-year-old Jeb home with him to join his own ten kids. If his wife Lula objected, Jeb never heard. She fussed over him and scolded him, making sure he minded his manners and did his share of chores. She also was the only person, much to his objection, who called him Jebediah.

There were few problems, until he started to school. He couldn't understand why Adam couldn't go with him. Lula explained that black children couldn't go to the white school. Jeb decided he would go to the black school, but quickly found out there wasn't one. He returned to the school for whites, still not understanding the problem.

At first, he took the name calling and unwelcomed punches. There was one boy in particular who delighted in tormenting Jeb. That ended the day Jeb punched him in the gut and broke his nose. The boy's father demanded that Jeb be expelled from school. He was ten years old at the time. During his short time in the education system, he learned to read, write a bit, and do his sums. He shared that knowledge with his adopted siblings.

Jeb often wondered how his life would have been if his uncle hadn't ridden in and taken him away a few weeks after being expelled from school. No sense dwelling on the past. He needed sleep.

Something awakened Jeb before sunrise. All was still and very cold. Lying quiet, he listened for any unusual sound and then glanced at Tulip and Brownie. They were looking to the east, but didn't seem disturbed. Jeb put on his hat, eased into his boots, and crept into the underbrush. There was little foliage so Jeb slipped from tree to tree, being careful not to step on a frozen stick or break a tree limb.

A familiar sound caught his attention and what came into view scared him. A line of horses, each carrying an Indian brave, walked in single file just beyond the timberline. The braves wore their hair cut blunt below the ears, parted in the middle, and held in place by some type of headband. The short, stocky men were wrapped in blankets over leggings, a breech cloth, and moccasins. All these characteristics shouted Apache to Jeb.

After the warriors passed, he backed carefully out of his hiding place and returned to camp. He checked on Russ and found the boy awake.

"You're up early," he said, not wanting to alarm him.

"Yes, sir," Russ answered. "Where are we going?"

"I'm taking you to stay with a friend of mine, until I can locate some of your kinfolks."

"I don't think I have any kinfolks."

Jeb didn't mention the Indians he had seen. "We'll worry about that later. Right now we need to eat and get moving."

After a breakfast of jerky and a cold biscuit, Jeb saddled Brownie and loaded up the pack. He set Russ behind the saddle, and then took a broken tree branch and made an attempt at brushing away signs that someone had camped there. It might fool a white man, but he knew no Indian would fall for the trick.

The problem now was getting out of the area without running into another band of braves. Indians moving meant the weather was going to improve. If one bunch was on the move, there would be others.

To avoid more travelers Jeb hugged the timber line, traveling through muck and fallen limbs. He rode tense and alert. After about two hours, he thought it safe to stop and fix something to eat. Mostly, he wanted a cup of strong, black coffee.

Russ searched about for more wood, while Jeb started a fire under an overhang in a gulley. The smoke would be blocked by the overhang, as long as the fire was small. Although a good-sized fire would chase away the chill, he decided he'd rather be cold than dead.

The sun brightened in the east, promising welcomed warmth.

"Looks like we may have a decent day," Jeb said, still nursing a cup of coffee.

Russ didn't comment.

"You okay?" Jeb asked.

Tears rolled down Russ' cheeks. He looked up with big blue eyes. "I miss my ma and pa."

"I know you do, and I wish I could bring them back for you. But I can't. The best I can do is get you somewhere safe. Right now, I think a good place for you is with some people I met just before I found you. I'd best explain that these folks are Creek Indians. You've no cause to like

Indians, but these are far different from the Comanches that killed your folks. Instead of raiding and killing, the Creeks raise crops. They don't go off terrorizing people. They stay close to home and take care of their own. Now, understand they will fight if needs be."

Russ sucked in a deep breath. "I want to stay with you."

"I'm a Texas Ranger on the trail of an outlaw named Burris. I'll make a deal with you. You stay with these folks, until I get Burris behind bars or hung. Then I'll come back for you. I can't risk taking you on the chase for fear of getting us both killed."

"You promise you'll come back?"

"I'll be back, but it may be a spell before I catch up to Burris."

That having been said, Russ focused on eating. When he finished, he took Tulip a piece of a biscuit.

Jeb sat with his coffee and pondered the situation. By his estimation, they would reach the trading post late in the day. Perhaps it would be better to kill some time here and arrive in the morning. No, he was stalling. Best get on with it before he decided to take Russ with him.

The sun was well above the horizon by the time they broke camp.

It wasn't long before the ground started to thaw. Brownie made his way through the muck, slipping a few times.

Late in the afternoon the trading post came into view. Jeb took a deep breath and nudged Brownie to keep moving. He noticed Russ grow tense as they approached the post.

"It will be okay," Jeb assured him.

Until now it hadn't occurred to Jeb that Fooswah might not keep the boy. Well, if she wouldn't maybe Owen would.

Whatever happened he would make sure Russ was safe.

* * * * *

CHAPTER 7

JEB reined in Brownie on a hill that overlooked a worn wood building.

From this view the trading post sat like the hub of a wagon wheel with spoke-like trails running from it in all directions.

Individual dwellings dotted the landscape around a large clearing that surrounded the important building. At this time the clearing was filled with men, women, and children.

"Are they on the warpath?" Russ asked.

"I don't see any warpaint or weapons. I think we're safe." Although Jeb felt that was true, he took the thong from his pistol. "Let's see what's going on."

When they reached the edge of the clearing, the crowd opened a path to the hitching rail. As Brownie and Tulip progressed, the people filled in behind and around them. Jeb's attention was drawn to a big red-headed man pacing like a caged bear back and forth on the front porch.

"Owen, are you trying to wear out the boards?" Jeb shouted.

"Did you catch that murdering breed?" Owen asked.

"Not yet, but I will."

"Then what are you doing back here?"

"I need to talk to Fooswah."

"You came back to visit and let that murdering snake get away?"

"Owen, what's troubling you? Calm down, and I'll explain."

"My wife's been in labor for hours. I'm afraid she's in trouble, and there's no doctor to help her."

"Has she had trouble in the past?"

Before Owen could answer, a big cheer went up from the crowd. He jumped off the porch and ran to a nearby cabin. He was not allowed to enter, but when he turned away he was smiling.

"I have a son!" he announced to Jeb.

"Congratulations! I'll buy you a drink."

With Russ in tow, the men went inside the building. Wonderful warmth greeted them. Although the sun had been shining, it was still bone chilling cold outside.

Approaching the boy, Owen stuck out a big paw. "I'm Owen."

Russ stammered his name and shook the man's hand.

Owen turned to Jeb. "I suppose you have a good excuse for letting Burris get away."

"Burris might as well hang hisself, because I intend to see that it's done," Jeb said. "He and his cronies killed Russ' ma and pa."

Owen laid his hand on Russ' shoulder. "I'm sorry young'un. That's a bitter dose to swaller. They killed my oldest boy, so I know how you feel." He looked at Jeb. "How can I help you?"

"I thought Fooswah might let Russ stay with her until I catch Burris. I can't very well take him with me. It's too dangerous."

"Fooswah is here helping my wife, Morning Star. You talk to her and see what she says. I'd help you out, but I've already got five kids. No, make that six." Owen looked at Russ. "You two are probably hungry. I'll have Hoktee, my sister-in-law, bring you some stew."

Jeb nodded. "We'd be much obliged."

A short, chubby Indian girl brought out two bowls of stew and several pieces of frybread. Jeb and Russ got down to business.

"What kind of bread is this?" Russ asked between bites.

"It's called frybread. Mighty good, ain't it?"

"Shore is."

Russ rubbed his full belly and sighed. After nodding off for a minute, he jerked awake. "Can I go check on Tulip?"

Jeb nodded, and then headed toward the door. He smiled to himself when he noticed the piece of frybread Russ had stuck in his pocket. Together they took Brownie and Tulip to the lean-to.

Russ took great pains brushing the fuzzy little burro and checking her hooves. He gave her the bread and hugged her goodnight. "Maybe I'd better sleep out here with Tulip."

"You can if you want to. Matter a fact, I'll sleep out here too. But first I want to talk with Fooswah."

"Want me to go with you?" Russ asked.

"No, not just yet. I'll come get you if I need you."

As Jeb entered the room, Fooswah was visiting with Owen. With Owen translating, Jeb explained the situation.

Fooswah asked how she was supposed to feed an extra mouth, especially that of a growing child.

"I'll gladly pay for whatever you need," Jeb said. "Have Owen keep a tab for me."

"Where is this child?" Fooswah asked.

As Jeb left to get Russ, he almost knocked him out with the door.

"Come on in," Jeb told him.

Fooswah looked Russ over carefully, even so far as checking his teeth. "Does he know work?"

"I'm sure he does. Russ, are you willing to help out with chores and not be a burden?"

"Yes, sir."

"Talk in the morning," Fooswah said.

"I know you're not happy about this," Jeb said, as he and Russ walked to the lean-to. "I hope you'll trust that it's the best for you right now."

"I trust you, but I'm scared."

"What would make you feel better?"

"I'd feel better if Tulip could stay with me."

Jeb was stunned. "Okay, you can keep Tulip, if you promise to take good care of her."

Russ smiled. "I'll protect her with my life."

"Well, that probably won't be necessary. Just make sure she has plenty of fresh water and a bite of oats or corn every day. I'll explain all of that before I leave. Fooswah hasn't decided to keep you, yet. Right now, we'd best get some shut-eye."

"Jeb, Fooswah has funny-colored eyes. Is something wrong with her?'

"No, she is a white woman who was taken by Comanches years ago. She escaped, and the Creeks took her as one of their own."

"So, does that make her a white Indian?"

"I suppose. Now get some sleep."

"I can't talk Indian."

"You'll learn," Jeb assured him. "And maybe Fooswah will begin to remember English."

"Thanks for saving me."

"You're welcome. I'm just sorry I couldn't save your folks."

"Jeb, I was awful scared when we rode in the middle of those Indians. My teeth were chattering."

"Well, I was drawed up tighter than a fiddle string myself. Go get your buddy and curl up with her so you can sleep."

Curled up next to his burro friend, Russ slept while Jeb cleaned his weapons and worried over what the morning would bring.

* * * * *

CHAPTER 8

DAYLIGHT found Jeb making his way to the trading post, hoping for a cup of coffee.

Owen welcomed him by filling a cup with steaming brew. "Where's the boy?"

"Still asleep. Didn't see any need to wake him just yet."

Fooswah entered the room and joined the men at the table.

She took a sip of coffee and began speaking to Owen, who in turn translated what she said to Jeb.

"She's decided not to keep the boy. Said she's too old and has had much bad luck with children. Her three died young."

"Well, I guess I'll take him with me."

Suddenly, a loud ruckus erupted outside. Owen, Jeb, and Fooswah rushed out the door.

An older Indian boy and Russ were arguing and circling each other. The bigger boy punched Russ in the mouth. The little redhead spit out blood, and then charged like a raging bull. He rammed his head in his opponent's stomach, knocking the wind out of him. When he doubled over and fell to the ground, Russ jumped on top of him and went to work with his fists. The older boy struggled for air and tried to defend himself.

Russ continued punching, until Jeb pulled him off the Indian boy.

"What's this all about?" Jeb demanded.

Russ wiped blood from his mouth. "He pulled Tulip's ear. She bit him. Then he hit her with a stick."

Owen spoke to the other boy, who as it turned out was one of his sons. "I'm sorry about that, Jeb. The boy knows better."

Russ went to Tulip and checked her over. "She's alright."

"Owen, I need to get a few things, and then we'll head out." Jeb turned back to the trading post.

Fooswah said something that made Owen laugh.

"What's so funny?" Jeb asked.

"She says she'll keep Little Wasp."

"What made her change her mind?"

Owen scratched his beard and grinned. "I guess she likes a scrapper.

Don't question her decision."

Russ washed his face and hands before entering the trading post. Jeb and Fooswah, after checking him over, decided he would survive.

Owen looked at the list, which included Jeb's supplies and frowned. "You're running up quite a bill."

"I'll pay with the money I get for Burris. In the meantime, let Fooswah get what she needs." Jeb picked up a bolt of bright red cloth. "Give me a couple of yards of this and the same of the blue."

As they headed out the door, Jeb noticed a double-barrel shotgun standing in the corner. "That gun for sale?"

"Where you going to carry it?" Owen questioned.

"I'm not. I'm getting it for Russ and Fooswah. I'll teach them to use it before I leave."

"Dad-blame, man," Owen grumbled, "I just put your tally sheet in the safe. Are you sure you're through buying?"

"I'm through. I'll get loaded up and out of your hair. Sure appreciate your hospitality. Come on, Russ, let's get moving."

Man, boy, and woman made their way toward Fooswah's cabin, which was a couple of miles north of the trading post.

Jeb had lost a lot of time, but felt he could pick up Burris' trail again. Although he hated to leave Tulip, it was probably best. The little burro didn't travel very fast. Jeb's method of catching bad guys in the past had been to dog their trails, until they got tired of him and turned back after him. This time was different. He wanted to catch Burris before he killed again, and then return for Russ. Funny how in a short time he had grown so fond of the boy.

Once at the cabin, they unpacked supplies. Jeb smiled when Fooswah found the cloth.

She smoothed it with her hands. "Mado." *Thank you.* After carefully folding the material, she put it in a trunk at the end of the bed and went to the kitchen area.

While Fooswah cooked, Jeb explained to Russ that without being told, he should always make sure the water bucket was full and that there was kindling in the box by the stove.

The lean-to for the horses was a mess, so man and boy went to work mucking out horse manure. Jeb stored the corn and oats he'd bought, and then demonstrated the amount to be fed.

"Tulip will eat until she explodes, so never leave the lid open to the corn bin," Jeb warned. "Don't feed her a bunch of bread. Just a treat now and then."

"She sure likes bread."

"I know, but you don't want a sick burro, do you?"

"No, sir. I'll not feed her too much bread or corn."

"I know you'll take good care of her."

Satisfied that Russ knew how to care for Tulip and the horse Burris left, they made their way to the cabin.

Fooswah motioned for them to sit at the table. She had prepared venison steaks in a thick gravy.

Fry bread caught Russ' attention. The boy ate well, especially the bread. Jeb noticed that he didn't sneak any for Tulip.

They were busy the rest of the day unpacking and arranging a place for Russ to sleep. Jeb figured the boy would spend most nights in the lean-to with Tulip, which was what he did when the evening shadows appeared.

"Jeb, are you sure you'll come back?" Russ asked.

"Sure as shooting, but it may be a while. I have a long way to travel before catching up with Burris. Once I find his trail, I have to corner him and haul him to the nearest jail or fort. Try not to worry about me. Do your best to help Fooswah. Indian children are treated well. Never heard of any being mistreated. You'll be fine."

"But I ain't Indian."

"Don't matter. You're a young'un."

"I'm going to miss you."

"I'll miss you, too, but it's what's best."

* * *

JEB awakened at first light. He tried to be quiet, as he led Brownie out of the lean-to.

Jerking awake, Russ jumped to his feet. "Are you leaving?"

"It's time. I'll see you when the job's done."

Before Jeb knew it, a small boy was wrapped around his legs, clinging to him. He picked up Russ, hugged him close for a minute, and then set him down.

Fooswah stood beside the boy, placing a gentle hand on his shoulder.

Jeb rode away, cussing himself for the tears in his eyes. Perhaps he was getting old, going soft. Finally, he looked back to see woman, child, and burro watching him. He raised his hand in farewell.

Fooswah and Russ waved, as Tulip brayed.

Fort Sill would be Jeb's first stop. If the outlaw had been in the area, someone would have seen or heard of him. Since Burris was riding with others, capture might not be easy. Then again, it seldom was. Meanwhile,

Jeb needed to keep a sharp eye and concentrate. He was riding into the heart of Indian Territory, home to some mighty mean folks. Daydreaming would get him killed, so he'd best put on his ranger hat.

With that thought, he lifted his hat and put it back on more firmly.

* * *

AFTER Jeb rode west, Russ, Fooswah, and Tulip walked a half-mile to put out throw lines on the North Canadian River.

The river was up and running fast from the recent snow and rain. With caution they made their way down a slippery bank to the water's edge.

Russ watched Fooswah tie a line onto a limber willow pole she had cut. She demonstrated how to tie on the hook, bait it with a fat worm, and stick the pole in the mud so it stood almost straight up. The bait just barely dangled into the murky water. Russ doubted they would catch anything.

The day passed quickly. By evening Russ was lonesome for Jeb and wondered if he was thinking about them.

* * * * *

Part II

Lillian

CHAPTER 9

THE sun sank low in the western sky taking away light and warmth.

After putting out the fire, Jeb took his pack and moved a far distance into the trees. He may have been safe staying near the fire, but could not take the chance of a late traveler dropping by. It was cold after sunset. Jeb slipped deep into his bed covers and after a time became comfortable.

Brownie was tethered on a patch of dry grass near where Jeb slept. The sound of the horse cropping grass became a lullaby. He would continue to graze, unless something or someone disturbed him. If it stopped, his master would awaken.

By sunrise Jeb decided coffee and food could wait until the sun got higher, warming things up a bit. According to his calculations, he had over a hundred miles to travel. On a good day he could average twenty or maybe more, unless there were rivers to cross and Indians to avoid.

Once back on the move and not knowing exactly why, Jeb reined Brownie back toward the creek where he had found Russ. Perhaps he'd missed something in his haste to leave the area. It was a longshot, but it wouldn't hurt to have one more look.

Hunger compelled him to stop. He debated building a small fire. The desire for coffee prevailed. Jeb tied Brownie and loosened the cinch. After gathering wood, he kindled a small flame under the drooping limbs of a pecan tree and placed the coffeepot on a rock near the fire. In very little time bacon fried in the skillet, and the smell of coffee teased his senses.

Refreshed from his meal, Jeb made his way west. He traveled the beautiful spring day without seeing another human. That evening he camped near a small creek in a growth of willows.

After enduring another cold night, he headed toward the creek where the McQueery family had been attacked. He reached it by midday and eased along the edge of the timber. Brownie tensed and jerked up his head. Jeb reined him into the woods and hoped they hadn't been seen.

Brownie reacted to a loud screeching noise, almost unseating Jeb. Just as he got Brownie calmed down, it happened again. Jeb rode farther into the woods and tied Brownie to a tree. On foot he sought to find what was making the awful sound.

He couldn't believe his eyes, when he saw what was happening. A man stood on a fallen tree trunk sawing on a fiddle. A party of Indians sat on their ponies watching him. If one of the braves approached, the man drew the bow across the strings, upsetting the ponies. The man hollered at them, telling them to repent in one breath and calling them horrible names in the next. Jeb knew a well-aimed arrow would put an end to the fiddler. Then, wonder of wonders, the braves turned their mounts and rode away. Before Jeb could announce himself, the fiddle player fainted.

A splash of the ice-cold water from the creek revived the man in a flash. "Are you an angel?" he asked.

"No," Jeb replied. "Just passin' through and heard the commotion."

"I'm purely glad you did." He held out his hand. "Name's George Washington Scott."

"Jebediah Powers. What are you doing in this country?"

"I was with a wagon train headed to Texas, but the wagon master kicked me out."

"Wasn't because of your music, was it?"

George scowled. "No. He made inappropriate comments to Miss Vaughan. I suggested that he apologize to her. He suggested I take a hike. He kicked out a family about five or six days ago, so I decided to try and find them. They're nice folks, who I figure will let me trail along with them. Name's McQueery."

"They're buried down the creek a ways. Indians killed them and burned their wagon."

The young man dropped to his knees and began to pray for their safe journey to heaven.

"We'd best be moving," Jeb said. "Where's your horse?"

"Don't have one. The wagon master, Tom Stacy, kept him and my belongings. All I managed to save was my violin."

"Where were you when you left the wagon train?"

"About five miles from here, I reckon. After the McQueerys left, one of the wagons lost a wheel. Then Mr. Allford was hurt trying to fix it. The animals were about done in, so Stacy said we'd rest for a few days."

"Let's go get your horse."

"He's a mean man," George warned, "and much bigger than you."

"That will make it more fun. Come on. We'll take turns riding and walking."

"I'm in your debt."

"Not yet. Before this is over, we may both be walking. Do me one favor. Don't be sawing on that fiddle."

George Washington laughed. "I'll play you a proper tune one of these days."

Jeb wondered how the wagon train missed being attacked by Indians. Perhaps they had chosen the McQueerys, who traveled alone with little or no defense.

"How many are in the wagon train?" Jeb asked.

"Six wagons."

"Did you have any Indian trouble?"

"No. I'd not seen an Indian until today."

"You'll probably meet some more before you get to Texas."

"I sure hope not."

A little before sunset campfires from the wagon train came into view.

"We'll camp here tonight," Jeb said. "Then speak with Mr. Stacy in the morning. If you'll gather firewood, I'll take care of Brownie and get the coffeepot."

Both men were exhausted. They ate supper and crawled into their blankets. George Washington's, however, was a borrowed horse blanket, but he seemed grateful for it.

* * *

THEY arrived at the wagon train about daylight. Tom Stacy rode out to meet them.

"He's riding my horse," George said.

"Can't say as I blame him. That's a mighty fine animal."

"He is one of the finest thoroughbreds in Virginia."

"What are you doing back? I told you to hit the road!" Stacy glared at George and then turned to Jeb. "Who are you?"

"Name's Jebediah Powers. Give this man back his horse."

"You going to make me?"

"If necessary."

"Well, I guess it's necessary. Guns, fists, or knives?"

"Fists will work. It'll be a pleasure to give you a whipping."

Both men dismounted, unbuckled their gun belts, and walked toward each other. By this time, folks from the wagons had gathered to see what was happening.

Jeb questioned his decision, as Stacy approached. The man must have weighed close to two-hundred pounds and stood about six feet tall. Jeb weighed maybe one-fifty and was only five-feet-ten.

Stacy swung a hard right at Jeb's face. Jeb ducked under the punch and hit Stacy in the gut. The big man slowed a bit, perhaps surprised by the smaller man's strength. Stacy stormed in to catch Jeb in a bear-hug, but the agile man slipped from his grasp and slugged him in the mouth. Stacy swung and staggered Jeb with a hard right to the head. While still seeing stars, Jeb ducked and dodged until his head cleared a little. Thinking he was winning, the big man charged again, but was met by a left to the head and a right to the belly. He stumbled, almost fell, and struggled to get his bearings. Jeb gave him another right to his middle and a left to the mouth. Stacy went down and stayed there.

"Get your horse and belongings," Jeb said to George.

"Look out!" a woman hollered.

Jeb turned. As Stacy came at him with an axe, George tossed Jeb his pistol. He snatched it out of the air and pointed it at Stacy. "Drop it, or I'll kill you dead."

Stacy dropped the axe and stomped away from them.

George introduced Jeb to Lillian Vaughan.

As usual, Jeb was tongue-tied around women, but he finally managed to thank her for the warning. He didn't know how to respond, when George told her about the McQueery family.

"Did they kill that sweet little boy?" she asked.

"Are you going to Fort Sill?" George asked.

Jeb appreciated the quick save. "That's the plan, but sometimes plans get changed sudden like."

"Can I ride along with you?" George asked. "I promise I won't be any trouble."

Lillian stepped closer. "Oh, please, can I come too? That horrible man scares me."

Jeb nodded. He couldn't believe he had just agreed to take a fiddle player and a beautiful lady with him.

He pointed to George. "You are not to touch that instrument, until we reach Fort Sill." Then he pointed to Lillian. "And you are not going to complain. If you can't keep up, you'll be left behind. What about your belongings?"

"Oh, I'll keep up," she replied. "I was raised in a saddle. I'll leave my belongings in the Smith's wagon. I was traveling with them to Fort Sill."

Jeb gave a sigh of relief that she hadn't mentioned Russ again. If she did, what would he tell her?

* * * * *

CHAPTER 10

GEORGE Washington rode to the cottonwood tree.

"Give me your hat," Jeb ordered.

Looking confused, George handed his black hat to Jeb, who started to remove the headband.

"What are you doing?" George asked.

"Getting rid of those flashy conchos that can be seen for miles. If you have any other shiny objects on your person or tack, get rid of it." He turned to Lillian. "Same goes for you. We'll be lucky to get out of this country with our hair without calling attention to ourselves. No talking, singing, or fiddle playing. Stay close, but in single file. If I tell you to do something, don't question. Just do it. Let's move."

Jeb stayed close to the timber. They traveled until well past noon, and then stopped to let the horses rest.

"I'll gather some wood," Lillian said, picking up a couple of sticks.

"No. We'll do without a fire until we find a better place. If you're hungry, there's jerky in my saddlebag."

Shortly before sunset, they reached the South Canadian River.

"We'll camp here for the night," Jeb announced. "Then cross in the morning."

Lillian looked at the meandering water from a high bank at the river's edge. "How are we going to get to the water, much less cross it? It looks a mile wide."

"It's not quite a mile, but will seem like it. I'll look for a place to cross, while you two get some grub fixed. Best build your campfire in that low spot and make it small."

Lillian welcomed Jeb back with a cup of coffee and a plate of beans with a couple of slices of bacon on the side.

He finished eating and poured another cup of coffee. "I found a place where we can get to the water, but it's just an animal path. It's going to be rough to get through. Once at the water, don't hesitate. Act scared, and your horse will sense it. Don't try to control him, and don't panic if the current takes you downstream a little. Hang on tight, but if your horse starts floundering, slip off and grab his tail so he can swim more freely.

When you get to the other side, don't tarry. Get to higher, drier ground. Watch for quicksand. This river is known for it."

"Mr. Powers, I can't swim," Lillian said.

"You won't have to unless your horse gets into trouble. Just remember, if you lose hold of the saddle don't fight the current. Let it carry you to the other side." He didn't tell her that he couldn't swim, either. "There's no need for Mr. Powers. Call me Jeb."

"Only if you'll call me Lillian."

"Sounds good to me," Jeb said. "It's going to be cold in the morning. Better to wrap your coat and extra clothes in your slicker and tie 'em tight behind your saddle. No doubt we'll get wet.

"Lillian, you take first watch. Wake George Washington in about three hours. He'll wake me in three hours, and I'll take it from there. Remember to watch the horses. They'll warn you in case of danger."

* * *

THE sun was barely up, when the trio made their way through a tangled mess of vines and trees.

At the river's edge, Jeb pulled up Brownie and waited for the others. He tied his rope to his saddle horn and pitched the loose end to Lillian.

"Dally the rope around your saddle horn," Jeb told her. "Don't tie it off. Just hold on to the end with your hand. George, you're on your own, but I'll help if you get in trouble."

"What does dally mean?" Lillian asked.

Jeb quickly demonstrated by taking the rope and making a couple turns around her saddle horn. "Hold on to the end of the rope. To get loose, all you have to do is let go."

"How can I hold the rope, my reins, and the saddle horn?"

"Tie the split reins together and let them hang loose on your horse's neck. You can't control your horse once he's in the water. Whatever happens, don't panic."

He guided Brownie into the water. Brownie struggled when he hit the swift, strong current. Lillian and her horse were right behind, and for a minute her big bay panicked.

"Don't fight him!" Jeb hollered. "He'll be okay."

The horse struggled some, but managed to swim to shallow water on the other side.

George ran into trouble about halfway across. He slipped out of the saddle and clung to the horn, but lost his grip and fell into the current. He turned onto his back and let the swift water carry him downstream. Jeb and Lillian watched him go around a bend and out of sight.

"Get his horse," Jeb told Lillian.

Wheeling Brownie, Jeb raced down the river's edge. He found George stranded on a sandbar.

"Hang on," Jeb told George. "I'll toss the rope and pull you across."

A few minutes later they were all together. Jeb noticed Lillian shaking from the cold air. "Get changed into dry clothes, and let's get moving. We've made enough noise to attract attention."

George pointed to the east. "There's smoke back across the river."

"The wagon train most likely. Let's ride. We'll change later." Jeb kicked Brownie into a lope.

Lillian caught up with him. "Aren't we going to go back to help them?"

"We'd have to cross against the current. Even if we made it, we'd be too late. Let's move." Jeb led off at a gallop.

They rode at a fast clip for half an hour and then pulled up to give the horses a breather. Jeb rode over a small hill into a grove of blackjack trees.

"George, shinny up that lone cottonwood and keep an eye on our backtrail. Lillian, get into some dry clothes, while I start a fire and brew coffee. We'll eat jerky again, because I don't plan to be here long."

"I need a boost to get up this tree," George said.

"Jump and grab a low limb," Jeb suggested. "Then pull yourself up."

"I'll try." After a couple of jumps, George managed to grab a limb, pull himself up, and climb higher.

When Lillian returned in dry clothes, Jeb handed her a cup of coffee and a piece of jerky. He left the area to change his own clothes, and then George came down from his perch to change.

Scrambling up the tree, Jeb took George's place. He knew there would be no visible dust this early in the day. They had better make tracks, because if the wagon train had been attacked the Indians would be moving fast. They might come this way. There was no way of knowing. He glanced up one more time, preparing to climb down.

A group of riders raced across the countryside, heading their way.

Jeb dropped to the ground. "Get the horses deeper into the woods and grab your rifles. We may have company we don't want."

"Can't we make a run for it?" George asked.

"No. Right now they may not know we're around. I doubt they've taken time to do much tracking. Let's hope they didn't cross the river where we did. If we're lucky, they will head north or south away from the direction of the fort. Lillian, can you shoot?"

"Yes."

"George, how about you?"

"Never shot a gun in my life, so you'd best give me a quick lesson."

Jeb grabbed his rifle and explained. "When you work this lever, it puts a shell in the chamber. Site down the barrel and squeeze the trigger. Then work the lever again. Keep doing that until you run out of bullets."

"Lillian, get behind those fallen trees over there. George, get behind that dirt mound. I'll get behind a tree on my left. If they head this way, we'll open fire. I'll tell you when to cut loose."

"Jeb," George said, "I don't think I can shoot a person."

"They won't think twice about killing you. We need to protect Lillian. Say a prayer and get ready. Here they come."

George shuddered. "Our Father—"

"Pick out the closest one," Jeb interrupted, "and lay the lead to him."

The five braves were caught off guard. Two fell immediately, and another was wounded. They wheeled their ponies and took off.

"Will they be back?" Lillian asked.

"Not unless they gather some help. We put the scare in them, but we need to get away from here."

"Jeb, would you take a look at my leg?" George asked.

"What's wrong with it?"

"It has an arrow stuck in it."

Sure enough, George had caught an arrow in his right leg.

"Lillian, heat some water and bring me that bottle of whiskey from my saddlebag." Jeb tied his bandana above the arrow. "George, I've got to break the arrow before pushing it on through. Take a slug of whiskey and brace yourself."

George took a good pull from the bottle. "Do it!"

Jeb broke the arrow near the feathered end and pushed it on through George's calf. Lillian bathed the wound with warm water, poured some whiskey on his leg, and then bandaged it with strips of cloth torn from her blouse tail.

"We have to get him in the saddle," Jeb said. "Help me."

Together they got George mounted.

"I'm afraid he's going to pass out," Lillian said.

"We'll tie him in the saddle. Every minute we're here puts us in danger. Might have been Kiowas. Whoever they were, they don't take kindly to whites being in their country."

* * * * *

CHAPTER 11

"LILLIAN, you ride drag and keep an eye on our back-trail. I'll try to get us out of here. Hang in there, George."

Jeb stayed near the timber as much as possible. They only crossed open country when necessary. At least the sun was shining, which warmed their chilled bodies.

Lillian kept watch behind them and on George, who rode slumped in the saddle. His right leg hung loose instead of in the stirrup.

When Lillian noticed blood dripping from his leg, she caught up to Jeb. "George's leg is dripping enough blood to leave a trail."

"We'd best have a look." Jeb turned Brownie into a thicker area of trees. "Scatter some dirt over the blood. It probably won't fool anybody, but we'll give it a try. Catch up when you finish."

Twisting and turning through the trees, Jeb finally found a possible hiding place. It was a chance he had to take.

"I'll water the horses," Lillian offered.

"Okay. Keep a sharp eye out."

Lillian led the horses to a nearby creek, where they drank their fill. She tied them, took the canteens, and went upstream to fill them.

Jeb came to her. "He's losing blood fast. I'm going to have to find a way to stop the bleeding, or he won't make it. Do you have anything metal we can stick in the hole the arrow made?"

"Would a hat pin work?"

"It might. Let me see it."

Lillian took the pin from her hat and handed it to Jeb. "I'll stay near the horses, unless you need me to help."

"I think I can handle it. You stand guard."

Once back with George, Jeb started a fire. "I'm going to get this red hot and sear the inside of the hole in your leg. It's going to hurt like hell. If I don't do it, you'll bleed to death."

"Won't a tourniquet work?"

"If we were close to the fort and a doctor, it would. Beings how we're miles away, you'd risk losing your leg."

"Might need to give me another slug of whiskey."

Once the hat pin was red hot, Jeb handed George the bottle. He took a healthy drink just before Jeb thumped him on the head with the butt of his pistol, knocking him out cold.

"Sorry, George, but I can't have you hollering."

As quickly as possible, he ran the hot pin along the sides of the hole in George's leg. He reheated the pin, did it a second time, and then waited for the bleeding to stop. The problem now was moving him.

Jeb left George and went to Lillian. "He can't ride. If his leg starts bleeding again, he'll most likely die."

"What are we going to do? We can't leave him."

"Our only chance is for me to get to the fort as quickly as possible. Which means leaving you both."

"I'd rather not, but it makes sense. How long will you be gone?"

"A few days, if I don't run into trouble. I'm going to take the horses, so I can change often and travel fast. If anyone finds our tracks, they'll hang with me and pass right on by you."

"I'm scared."

"I am, too," Jeb admitted. "But I don't know any other way without risking George's life. That arrow could have had a poisoned tip. He may still die."

"Well, let's not dwell on the pitfalls. I could use a cup of coffee laced with a shot of whiskey. Care to join me?"

Lillian poured coffee for them both and added a generous amount of whiskey. She and Jeb sipped their drinks in silence. When Jeb finished his coffee, he took bedrolls and saddlebags off the horses.

"Will we have enough food to last?" Lillian asked.

"You'd better be sparing. Cook once a day over a small fire and away from where you're camping. Best you don't have a fire at night."

"Is this a good place to stay?"

"As good as any around here. Let's get George moved into that bunch of willows. I'll cut out some brush, but not so's you'd notice. Think you can help me get him in there?"

Lillian turned toward where George lay. "I'll do my best."

Together they half-carried, half-dragged the unconscious man into the willows. Jeb cut away enough in the middle of the clump of slender trees to make a place for George. While Lillian used his knife to cut a place for herself, Jeb carried in saddlebags and bedrolls. It didn't take long to gather everything they owned.

"What can I do to help him?" Lillian asked.

"Make some broth from a piece of jerky and let him sip it. If fever hits him in a day or two, bathe him with cold water. If he gets crazy and starts fighting, knock him out with the gun butt."

"I don't think I can hurt George."

"You might be saving his life and yours. If he starts raising cane and making noise, anyone close will hear him."

"Do you really think there are Indians nearby?"

"I don't know it for a fact, but I'd lay odds they'll be passin' through most anytime."

"I'll be careful. You do the same. When you get to the fort, look up my fiancé, Captain Webster. He'll help you."

"I surely will," Jeb promised. "Looks like rain clouds in the southwest. I need to get across the Washita River before the storm hits. Oh, here's a fish hook in case you have to scramble for food. There's worms under most any rotten wood. Remember to cook away from your camp and to find a spot where the smoke will filter through vines or tree limbs. Scatter the ashes and try to hide any evidence."

Jeb gathered the reins of the two extra horses and mounted Brownie. "I'll be back."

* * *

THROUGH tear-filled eyes, Lillian watched Jeb disappear into the mist.

With a deep breath she slipped into the maze of willows to check on George. He moved in his sleep, grimaced, and tried to sit up. Lillian propped him up against the bedrolls and then held a canteen to his lips.

He drank a little. "Where's Jeb?"

"He's gone to get help."

"Lord, how many days will he be gone?"

"I don't know," she admitted. "A few, I suppose."

"Let's get out of here. I can ride. Where's my horse?"

"Jeb took the horses, so the Indians wouldn't spot us. And so he could take turns riding them. We'll be fine as long as we stay still and quiet."

"Well, you might be fine, but I'm getting out of here." George tried to get to his feet. He winced and then passed out cold.

Lillian tied his hands and his feet. "You just saved yourself another headache."

She settled down beside George with canteen and pistol close at hand, and nodded off.

Voices awakened her. Someone was out where the horses had been tied. After what seemed like hours, she heard horses leaving in a run.

Jeb was right. They followed him.

* * *

JEB threw caution to the wind and raced across open country.

He rode Brownie first and then switched to the big thoroughbred. When he felt him begin to tire, he stopped to put a saddle on Lillian's bay. He had left her sidesaddle with her. It was tempting to rest a bit and maybe brew a cup, but something told him to keep going.

The sun was setting and storm clouds moving when he reached the Washita River. He didn't have much time until dark, but he needed to give the horses a rest. The river wasn't wide, but it had high banks and deep water. He wasn't looking forward to crossing with three horses. It would be better to wait until morning, but it looked like rain coming soon. He'd have some coffee and a bite of jerky. Things always looked better after a cup of coffee.

Plans changed when he saw a cloud of dust behind him.

After looping a rope between the two spare horses, he jumped into the saddle. In a mad dash he hit the river. The current wasn't as bad as the Canadian, and the horses swam across without difficulty.

Jeb found a creek running into the river and rode upstream through the water, hoping to cover his tracks. When it changed direction, he left the water and made his way to a stand of timber on a small hill. By that time it was dark. The horses were beat and so was he, but he unsaddled each one and gave them all a rub down. They found a bit of dry grass and started grazing. Despite the risk, Jeb built a small fire and put on the coffeepot. He didn't have anything to cook and at this point didn't care. His thoughts drifted to George and Lillian. She was tough and would make it. He wasn't sure about George.

The storm hit around daylight. Jeb donned his slicker and mounted Brownie. He was unsure about his location, but thought the fort lay to the southeast. He rode all morning in the rain, switching horses about every hour. If his calculations were right, he should make it to the fort by late that afternoon or early the next the morning.

The country was flat, except for a few rolling hills and sporadic stands of timber. Jeb rode across an open stretch and made his way along a creek. He was almost to the end of the timber line, when Brownie snorted and jumped to his right.

An Indian came off the ground, jumped, and caught him, pulling him out of the saddle. Jeb managed to tackle the man before he could get on Brownie. They went to the ground in a heap, and then both leaped to their feet. Jeb grabbed for his pistol, but the thong held it in the holster.

By this time the brave was charging with a drawn knife. Jeb drew his knife with the cutting edge up. The two circled each other. The brave rushed toward him and stabbed at him. Jeb knocked his arm to the side. This became the pattern, circle and jab for what seemed like hours. They were both bleeding from a few spots, but nothing serious.

Bone weary and tired of being on edge, Jeb decided to act. When the brave charged, Jeb caught his arm and pulled him forward, causing him to lose his balance and slide in the mud. Jeb rushed to meet him and threw a hard right to the brave's face. The blow stunned the Indian, giving Jeb time to release the thong from his pistol. He drew the gun and shot the Indian in the chest. He should have used his knife. That gunshot would bring every Indian in the country this way.

Exhausted, Jeb dropped to the ground. After resting for a moment, he walked to the brave to make sure he was dead. There was some kind of necklace around his neck. He jerked it off the man and put it in his pocket. He would look at it later.

The horses grazed nearby. He gathered their reins and climbed into the saddle. Indians or not, he needed to stop, eat, and rest. After riding another hour, he found a good spot and mostly fell out of the saddle. He somehow managed to unsaddle the horses and tether them close to water from a nearby creek.

A couple of cups of coffee and a broth cooked from jerky made him think he might just live.

Before he put out the fire, he took the necklace from his pocket. It was a locket. When he opened it, a small red-headed boy sitting on a lovely woman's lap looked back at him.

It was Russ and his mother.

* * * * *

CHAPTER 12

JEB'S mind spun with thoughts of George, Lillian, and a pretty woman holding a small boy.

Finding that locket had convinced him he was on Burris' trail. It was possible the killers had split up with the brave who jumped him.

As ever, his thoughts returned to Lillian.

"Some soldier is a lucky man," he whispered to himself.

The sun was higher than it should be when Jeb, bone weary, stirred to life. He didn't take time to make coffee. If his direction was correct, he hoped to reach the fort in an hour or two.

Gathering the horses, he saddled Brownie and then the bay. They both seemed in good shape. The thoroughbred, however, looked thin and worn out. Hopefully, the horse could make it to the fort, if Jeb didn't ride the haggard animal. He turned to check the cinch before mounting.

Suddenly, Brownie's ears perked up, and his head turned to the east.

Two deer bounded across an opening Jeb had intended to cross. Something or someone had scared the does.

Jeb led the horses deeper into the woods and watched the distant timberline. It wasn't long before a line of about fifteen braves rode from the woods into the clearing. Prepared for battle, they wore warpaint and carried shields, lances, bows, and arrows.

Once the last warrior disappeared from view, Jeb mounted Brownie and followed. Maybe he could warn whoever they planned to attack. He had to stay out of sight, which meant taking the least traveled route. After riding for an hour or so, Jeb came to a good-sized hill. He tied the horses, walked partway up, and then crawled to the crest.

Over the hill sat a small cabin with a barn and a corral. The Indians had spread out just far enough from the cabin to avoid notice.

Jeb rushed to the horses, mounted Brownie, and grabbed the lead ropes of the others. He raced up the hill and grabbed his rifle. Reaching the top, he gave a Texas yell followed by a series of gunshots. Then he made a mad dash toward the charging braves.

The cabin door flew open, but quickly closed. Jeb's warning gave enough time for someone to grab a rifle and begin firing from a loophole built into the cabin wall.

The battle ended as quickly as it began. Few of the warriors carried rifles, so they were overpowered without much difficulty. They left in a rush, taking only enough time to pick up two dead braves.

Out of the cabin came a young man. Dressed in homespun trousers complete with galluses, he was tall and stout with black hair and brown eyes. He walked toward Jeb with his hand extended. "I'm Harvey Simpson. I'm most thankful to you for saving my bacon. I didn't know there was an Indian within miles."

Jeb looked up at the man, who stood well over six feet. "Jeb Powers. I'm glad I happened along."

"Come in and meet my wife. She was in the midst of cooking breakfast, when all hell broke loose."

"I'll see to my horses and join you."

"I'll go with you. They could probably use a bait of corn."

"I'm sure they won't turn it down. We've been short on rations lately."

Harvey's wife Ellie was a pleasant-looking woman with light brown hair and blue eyes. A few freckles dotted her pale skin. She was tiny compared to Harvey, but Jeb had a feeling she could hold her own.

What impressed him most was the table she set. His mouth watered from the wonderful smells. He ate slowly, not wanting to appear ill-mannered. Between bites, he explained his situation to the Simpsons.

"You're several miles from the fort," Harvey informed him.

"This is new country to me. I need to get to the fort and send help for Lillian and George. Could I leave the thoroughbred and bay here? The big horse is about done in, not being used to such hard traveling. The bay belongs to Lillian, and I know she'd like to have him back."

"You bet. I'll take good care of them for you."

"Thank you. I'll tell them at the fort where to find the horses. Maybe they'll send someone for them, after they rescue Lillian and George."

"You think they're still alive?"

"Yes. Lillian is very capable and smart."

After one more cup of coffee, Jeb thanked Mrs. Simpson for the wonderful meal and shook Harvey's hand. He doubted the Indians would return, but warned Harvey to be alert.

Riding away, he found himself thinking that the Simpsons were lucky people to have a simple, but nice home in a lovely little valley.

Jeb rode in the direction Harvey gave him, all the while thinking about meeting Captain Webster, Lillian's fiancé. He would try to be open-minded but doubted he would think the man good enough for her. She was one of a kind, a woman to make a man proud. He hoped she'd be happy and wondered why he was concerned. He certainly didn't have time for a woman in his life, especially a woman already spoken for.

The fort came into view about mid-afternoon. Jeb rode in and asked a sentry where to find Captain Webster. After chasing around a bit, because the Captain was doing an inspection of quarters, Jeb finally found him.

"Captain Webster, I'm Jebediah Powers. I recently was in the company of your fiancée and a fellow named George Washington Scott."

"I thought Lillian was traveling with a wagon train coming here."

"She was. The wagon master, a man by the name of Stacy, frightened her. When I came along, she asked if she could ride with me to the fort. We also picked up George Washington Scott."

"Mr. Powers, let's go have a cup of coffee. I think I need to be sitting down when I hear the rest of your story."

"Just call me Jeb."

"Alright. Jeb it is."

After hearing the details about George and Lillian and the Indian attack on the Simpson place, Captain Webster jumped into action. In a matter of minutes he had a rescue team organized, that he would lead himself, and a patrol to search the area near the Simpson place.

"Can you go with us?" he asked Jeb.

Jeb knew he needed to keep after Burris, but felt seeing Lillian and George safe was more important. "Yes, Captain, I'll go."

After mapping out their route, Jeb, Captain Webster, and five soldiers left the fort. They took a wagon for George, an extra horse for Lillian, a couple of pack horses. At the last minute a doctor volunteered to join them. The captain figured to make ten miles before dark, but they only made about seven.

They made camp on a small hill near a stream running full of clear, cool water. The soldiers did most of the work, but Captain Webster also helped. Soon the horses were fed, watered, and on a picket line with a soldier guarding them. Horses were extremely important in this country, because they meant the difference between life and death.

Sentries were posted throughout the night, so for the first time in many days, Jeb slept soundly.

The next day they made excellent progress, until a wheel came off the wagon. A private unhitched the team and guarded them. While three men lifted the wagon, a fourth man shoved the wheel back into place. The next problem was finding a replacement for the pin missing from the hub of the wheel. One of the soldiers made a wooden peg from a stick of oak. It worked and they were on their way again, but not before losing a couple of hours of daylight.

On the third day, they reached Lillian and George. Both were alive but in bad shape from malnutrition and exposure to the elements. The doctor examined George's leg and thought he would be able to save it.

First order of business was a good meal, which Captain Webster prepared himself. Jeb was impressed when the man filled a plate, carried it to Lillian, and sat with her while she ate.

Damn. He didn't want to like him.

The next morning Lillian handed Jeb his fish hook. "I don't think I'll ever eat another finned creature, but I doubt we'd have survived without what I managed to catch. Thank you for taking care of us."

Jeb was stunned when she kissed him on the cheek. He turned to leave, but hesitated when Lillian mentioned the wagon train.

"Was the sweet little boy killed?" Lillian asked. "For some reason I feel you know, but aren't telling me."

"No, he wasn't harmed. I found him hidden in some willows and took him to live with a woman named Fooswah. She agreed to take him in until I can return for him and look for any kinfolks he might have."

"I'm so glad you found him. He is a lovely child."

With Lillian and George now safe, Jeb went his own way.

He rode off feeling a sadness he'd never experienced in his thirty-five years.

* * * * *

Part III

Fooswah

CHAPTER 13

RUSS jerked awake.

"Chabon, Chabon," someone called.

He jumped to his feet and ran outside the lean-to.

Fooswah stood on the porch and motioned for him to come.

Shivering in the cold morning air, he ran into the cabin behind her. The warmth of the kitchen felt mighty good, and the smell of bacon raised his spirits. The bacon was delicious, but the little cakes of something with honey poured on them were even better. He thought about saving one for Tulip. Remembering what Jeb told him, he just saved half of one.

Fooswah finished eating, scraped leftovers in a bucket, took her plate, and placed it in a large dishpan on the bench near the door. Russ followed her example, grabbed the water bucket, and headed to the creek. Thank goodness there was no ice that morning. The sun peaking over the horizon promised to be big and bright.

The full bucket of water was heavy. Russ used both hands to carry it and slopped water on his britches leg. He didn't know which was worse, toting a heavy bucket or a wet leg. A solution came to mind. He would only carry half a bucket and make more trips.

Fooswah took an old teakettle off the stove, poured hot water into the dishpan, and added a sliver of lye soap. She washed and rinsed each item, and then placed them on a clean rag to dry.

Russ carried in kindling and noticed that more needed to be cut. First, he had to feed Tulip and the horse.

When he returned from the lean-to, Fooswah was waiting for him. She turned and walked down the path that led to the river. Russ ran ahead to look over the high bluff that overlooked the water. Fooswah called to him and motioned him back. Within seconds there was a loud crash followed by a big splash. Part of the bluff had fallen into the river. If he had been at the edge, he would now be in the swift flowing water. Lesson learned.

They followed an animal path through vines, water willows, and trees to where Fooswah had placed the limb-line. The limb was dancing up and down. Russ grabbed the limb and pulled the fish to the bank. It was a nice catfish, almost more than he could handle. His doubts about her fishing abilities were gone. Fooswah rebaited the hook and stuck the limb again almost straight up at the water's edge. Russ understood now that the limb was placed that way so the fish couldn't pull it out of the mud. If it were angled toward the water, the fish would carry away both bait and pole.

Russ grabbed the big catfish and started up the path. He didn't get far, because the fish was much heavier than he had thought.

Appearing to sense his dilemma, Fooswah took the fish from him and hung it from a tree limb. She cut around the fins and gills, and then pulled the skin from the fish. Russ tried to help but wasn't strong enough. Finally finished, Fooswah rubbed her belly and smiled at Russ. He rubbed his belly and smiled back.

Tulip brayed from the lean-to, so Russ ran to check on her. She wanted out. Together boy and burro walked to the creek, Russ to get more water and Tulip to get a long drink.

"I'll brush you when we get back," Russ told Tulip.

The little animal bumped him with her head.

He didn't need to tether Tulip. She never strayed far. Not knowing what the horse might do, Russ tethered him on a long rope close to the creek, so he could drink as well as graze. So far, he had called the horse *Horse*. Maybe he should give him a name. All he came up with was outlaw, so Outlaw it would be, even though he was a very gentle fellow.

With Tulip on his heels, he carried the half-full water bucket to the cabin. Fooswah handed him a piece of bacon and a biscuit. He'd been so busy he hadn't realized he was hungry. Tulip looked so pitiful Russ laughed and gave her a bite of bread.

There was still kindling to cut. Russ picked up the hatchet and began cutting small strips of wood from a larger piece. It was a slow process. Thinking to move things along faster, he picked up the axe. He selected a spot to strike on the chunk of wood and swung the axe. His aim was off, causing the stick of wood to fly up and hit him in the forehead. Stunned, he reached up to check for blood. There wasn't anything wet, but he could feel a knot forming. He glanced toward the cabin, checking to see if Fooswah saw what happened. She wasn't in sight. Russ put down the axe and picked up the hatchet. He didn't want another knot on his head.

"Come on, Tulip," Russ said, walking to the lean-to. "I'll brush you. Tomorrow I have to clean this place. You and Outlaw sure poop a lot."

After brushing Tulip, he retrieved Outlaw and put him up for the night. Fooswah called for him.

Supper that evening was fried fish, some kind of corn dish, and frybread. Russ found himself wishing for a glass of milk. They always kept a milk cow at home. The fresh water was good, but not as satisfying as milk. He missed his old home and his ma and pa. Tears began to fill his eyes. He blinked several times and took another bite of frybread. The moment passed, but not the pain.

Needing something to distract him, he cleaned his plate and put it in the dishpan. Then he picked up the water bucket. It took five trips before filling the trough in the lean-to and the bucket in the cabin. When at last he went to the lean-to, he was one tired boy. He fell asleep curled up in a blanket next to Tulip.

Fooswah woke him just as the sun began to rise. He rubbed the sleep from his eyes, pulled on his britches, slipped into his shoes, and gave Tulip a hug. "See you in a minute," he told his friend.

Breakfast consisted of a strange mush, made tastier with honey. Russ left his bowl in the pan, picked up the empty water bucket, and headed to the creek.

There was a good supply of kindling. With that thought, he touched his forehead to see if the knot had gone away. Nope. Still there and pretty tender.

Fooswah left the cabin and headed toward the river. Russ ran to join her. They made their way to the limb line. There was no fish today and no bait. Fooswah grumbled to herself, baited the hook with a piece of bacon, and moved the line to a new spot.

Russ knew the task of cleaning the lean-to awaited him. He led Outlaw to an area where he could graze and made sure the lead rope was secure. Instead of joining Outlaw, Tulip decided to help. She blocked the door or bumped him, when he started to throw out a shovel full of manure.

He finally took her out and tied her to a tree limb. "You ain't helping, you crazy burro."

In about five minutes, she reappeared.

"I can't get my work done with you in the way." Russ led her back out and tied her more securely.

It took her about ten minutes to get loose the second time. Laughing, Russ chased her away. She ran circles around him and stayed just out of reach. He was about finished, so he put up the shovel.

After lunch, Fooswah left the cabin. Russ and Tulip joined her. They walked along a path that led in the direction of the trading post but turned off before getting to the post. In a short time, a small cabin appeared. Several children of various sizes played in the yard.

Fooswah said something to the children and then went into the cabin. Russ didn't know what to do. He sat on a stump, feeling like a stump himself. Tulip stood near him. The kids gathered around him, one daring to touch his hair, another to touch his hand.

Tulip allowed them to pet her, and one even tried to climb onto her back. She didn't like that.

All of the kids had big brown eyes, shiny black hair, and smooth brown skin. He wondered how their mother could tell them apart. The little ones scattered when an older boy approached. He said something Russ didn't understand.

"Hello," Russ said.

The boy smiled and motioned for Russ to follow him.

In a short time, they were in the woods back of the cabin. The Indian lad who called himself Osekee, which meant *Rain*, handed Russ a bow and an arrow. Russ had no clue what to do with the objects, but was willing to learn. Osekee taught him to nock the arrow, pull back, aim and release. Russ wasn't ready to go when Fooswah called for him.

When they arrived back at the cabin, he and Tulip headed to the lean-to, but Fooswah motioned for him to come inside. He didn't know what to do when she indicated he should remove his britches. She held up a blanket and turned her back to him, so he did as she asked. Peeking over the blanket Russ watched while she used his worn-out pants to make a pattern on some kind of material. In a short time, she handed them back to him.

Russ went to bed that night wondering when his new pants would be ready, and wishing he could tell Jeb about his archery lesson and that maybe he'd made a friend.

"Me and Tulip sure miss you," he said out loud. "Hurry back."

* * * * *

CHAPTER 14

"CATCH him!" Owen Hunter yelled. "Grab him by the leg!"

Russ didn't think yelling would make the task any easier.

Owen burst out laughing, when several pigs ran between Russ and Osekee. Even stoic Fooswah snickered a little.

Osekee finally caught a piglet by the back leg. The little animal squealed loud and long, frightening the boy so much he let it go.

"Why did you turn him loose?" Owen shouted.

"I hurt him," Osekee replied.

"No, you didn't. Pigs are squealers. Don't pay any attention to them."

"I don't like pigs," Russ proclaimed, as he attempted to catch one.

"You will this winter," Owen said, "when you smell bacon frying or ham baking."

With the help of some older boys, Osekee and Russ each caught two pigs to take home.

Owen gave away all but five of his sixteen piglets to the widows in the community. He also shared beef with them, when he butchered in the fall. They in turn provided his family with fresh vegetables in the summer.

The pigs were put in sacks, which were then tied together and tossed over Tulip. All the way home the pigs squealed and wiggled, causing Tulip to kick in agitation.

When they got home, Russ tugged Tulip toward the pen Fooswah's neighbors had built a few days ago out of stacked logs. He pulled the sacks off Tulip and one at a time opened them over the fencing. Once free the pigs became small red blurs, scampering around the pen.

Russ carried fresh water to them and emptied scraps into their wooden trough. They gobbled up the food and then rooted in the dirt. Russ decided he liked them a little better in their new home.

Fooswah came to the pen and nodded in satisfaction. She motioned for Russ to follow her to the cabin. He nodded back to her, and then held up the water bucket and turned toward the creek.

In a few minutes, he was seated at the table eating some kind of meat between two biscuits.

The language barrier made things difficult at times, but they were doing okay. A couple of times Fooswah called him Russ or close to it.

The sun was just above the horizon in the western sky, when Russ and Fooswah took their hoes and walked to a cleared area. They had worked for days getting the soil ready, so they could plant seeds Fooswah had saved from the previous year.

They toiled side-by-side until dusk, making the area larger. Then Russ went to feed the animals, while Fooswah fixed supper.

He fed Tulip and Outlaw. As he brushed Tulip, he explained why it was necessary for her to carry the sack full of squealers. Appearing to forgive him, she rubbed him with her head.

Before calling it a day, he checked on the pigs. The pen was empty.

Alarmed, he ran to the cabin. Fooswah finally understood his sign language, removed her apron, and followed him.

They found the critters at the edge of the creek rooting up all kinds of things to eat. Of course, Russ couldn't catch them and herding them was impossible.

Fooswah left and returned with a bucket of something. She gave the pigs a sniff of whatever it was and headed back to the pen. They ran behind her squealing like they were starving to death. After a quick survey of the fence, Russ found their escape hole. He fixed it the best he could and hoped they'd stay put.

Sunshine greeted Russ the next morning. Spring had arrived at last. First on his list of chores was the ever-empty water bucket. Thankfully, there was plenty of kindling. After breakfast he would feed the diggers and fix the hole better. This pig business might be a full-time job. He'd best hurry, because Osekee was coming over soon.

Meal over, Fooswah motioned for him to watch. She poured ground grain into the feed bucket, added water, and stirred it with a large, flat, wooden paddle. Russ understood this was pig feed, but it looked like what he'd eaten this morning. From Fooswah's hand signals, he knew he was to feed this to the pigs and bring back the bucket.

"Oh boy," he said to himself. "Another bucket to fill."

The pigs came running to greet Russ. When he started pouring the mush into their trough, they jumped in and got it all over themselves.

"You guys need to learn some manners."

A little later Osekee found Russ in the garden, helping Fooswah clear a larger area. He wanted to drop his hoe and go with his friend, but instead stayed to finish the job. Osekee took Fooswah's hoe and helped.

"Mado," she said to them and walked to the cabin.

Russ assumed *mado* meant *thank you*.

Together the boys went to the lean-to to let Tulip and Outlaw out to graze. Tulip greeted Osekee with a gentle butt to the arm. Osekee laughed and gave her a good rub. Once Outlaw was tethered on some grass, the youngsters grabbed fishing poles and a can of worms they had gathered in the garden. Along with a small burro, the boys raced off to the river.

They barely got out of the yard before two little pigs joined them. Russ came near to cussing. Osekee fell over laughing, while Tulip brayed her dislike for their company. Russ knew he couldn't drive them back, so he let just them stay.

Tulip grazed nearby, while the pigs rooted in the river sand and the boys fished. All were happy, especially when Osekee pulled in a large catfish. Russ wasn't far behind him. Together they caught seven nice fish. Osekee kept five because at his house there were several mouths to feed.

Wonder of wonders, the little pigs followed along with Russ and Tulip all the way to the cabin. Perhaps it was because of the fish Russ carried. Food always seemed to get their full attention.

Fooswah took clean clothes from the line as boy and animals came up the lane. She smiled, set down the basket, and indicated she would clean the fish. Russ nodded in agreement, because he had to get the pigs back into the pen and find their new escape route.

He found another hole, this time under the fence. The only thing he could find to fill it was sticks of firewood. Of course, the pigs wouldn't go into the pen until they spotted the bucket of feed.

"You guys need to stay in the pen," Russ scolded, as they attacked the food. "Something will eat you, if you keep getting out."

Evidently, the pigs didn't hear what Russ said, because they were out of the pen more than inside it.

Not knowing how to solve the problem, with Tulip at his side Russ went to the trading post and asked Owen Hunter for advice.

"I've heard about a type of wire we might try," Owen said. "I'll see if I can get some. In a day or two, I'll come over and put rings in their noses. That might help with the digging."

"How do you put rings in their noses?"

"With a pair of pliers. Watch for coyotes. They love pigs."

"Okay, let me know when you get the wire," Russ said.

"How are you and Fooswah getting along?" Owen asked.

"Just fine."

"That's good. I'm sure she's glad to have you."

"Thanks, Mr. Hunter. Be seeing you." Russ joined Tulip outside and headed home.

* * *

THAT night as they finished supper, coyotes howled and yipped.

"They're close." Russ grabbed the shotgun, but struggled to carry it.

Fooswah caught him going out the door and put a wadded-up towel under his shirt.

There was no way he could hold up the gun and aim, so he propped it up on the top log of the pen. The devils were getting closer. He could hear them sneaking through the brush, but couldn't see them.

"Come out, cowards," Russ yelled, his nerves shot.

That seemed to draw them closer. He pulled back the hammer on the right barrel, aimed the direction of the howling, and squeezed the trigger. The kick from the discharge knocked him down. When he was able, he checked but didn't find a dead coyote or any blood from one that he might have wounded.

The next evening, Russ and Tulip camped out by the pig pen. Tulip warned him when the coyotes were nearby. His arm was sore and turning purple. Dreading the thought of getting kicked again, he put more padding under his shirt.

Sure enough, the coyotes returned. A brave one dashed toward the fence. Russ took careful aim and squeezed the trigger, killing the coyote with one shot. Fooswah helped him drag away the varmint. They hung the dead animal from a tree limb as a warning to the others.

Fooswah motioned for Russ to come inside with her, but he shook his head no. He wound up sleeping with the pigs in the lean-to. The little critters climbed on him and rooted around on him. They were really cute, and he was determined they weren't going to be coyote food.

This became a nightly routine.

"I think Jeb would be proud of me, don't you?" Russ asked at breakfast, having shot and killed four coyotes.

He was surprised when Fooswah smiled and nodded.

* * * * *

CHAPTER 15

SIGNS of spring brought life to the drab countryside. Buds dressed the trees, promising green leaves to compliment the new growth beginning to pop up from the brown, dry, grass-covered soil.

Russ left the cabin, full from the big breakfast prepared by Fooswah. He breathed in cool, fresh air, as he carried the empty water bucket.

The pigs greeted him in anticipation of breakfast, but squealed their disappointment when he walked past their pen.

"I'll feed you in a minute. Maybe a little extra, since you stayed in the pen last night."

Water delivered and pigs fed, he headed to the lean-to. Russ carefully measured the feed for Outlaw and Tulip. While they ate, he brushed them and checked their hooves.

In a sudden mental flash, he decided to ride Outlaw. The horse was gentle, but Russ didn't know how he would feel about being ridden. There was only one way to find out. The saddle and bridle were stored in an empty manger. Russ got out the bridle with no trouble, but couldn't lift the saddle. The bit needed cleaning, but other than that was in good shape.

He was hard at work scrubbing the bit, when Fooswah came out of the cabin and walked over to see what he was doing.

"I'm going to ride Outlaw, but I can't lift the saddle," Russ said, as he walked to the lean-to.

Fooswah followed him to the manger. Even together they could barely budge the heavy saddle. Russ was puzzled when she walked back to the cabin. In a few minutes, she returned carrying a blanket of some sort. It was a heavy, canvas material with stirrups attached.

Russ indicated it lacked a horn. Fooswah reached up and took a handful of Outlaw's mane.

"Oh, I see," Russ said, picking up the bridle.

He approached Outlaw and tried to get the bit in his mouth, but the horse clamped his teeth together and raised his head. He tried several times without success. Finally, Fooswah took the bridle and demonstrated how to get him to take the bit. First, she showed Russ how to place his thumb in the corner of Outlaw's mouth. The horse opened his mouth far enough to slip in the bit. She also indicated not to hit his teeth by touching her own teeth and grimacing. The next problem involved getting the headstall over his ears. Many horses don't like their ears messed with, and Outlaw was one of them.

Again, Fooswah to the rescue. She unbuckled the headstall strap, put it behind the horse's ears, and then re-buckled it. Russ danced a little jig, which caused Tulip to run around making all kinds of noise. Fooswah covered her ears and laughed at the silly burro.

After Tulip calmed down, Fooswah lifted the canvas blanket and placed it on Outlaw's back. Russ wondered how it would stay on. His question was answered when Fooswah tied a surcingle over the blanket and around the horse. She then checked it to make sure it wouldn't pinch his front legs.

"Gosh, Fooswah. You sure know about horses. Thank you for helping me. I believe I'll get on him and see what happens." Russ gathered the split reins and prepared to climb aboard.

"No," Fooswah said, stopping him.

Taking the reins in her left hand, she put her left foot in the left stirrup and swung onto the horse's back, skirt and all. The elderly woman kicked Outlaw into a trot and then a gallop. She rode like a champion with head high, back straight, and no bouncing.

The boy stood mesmerized. She was awesome. He wanted to be able to ride and handle a horse just like she did.

Russ couldn't reach the stirrup, so Fooswah gave him a boost onto Outlaw's back. She took the reins and placed them in his hand, showing him how to hold them but not too tightly. Then she stepped back.

The horse remained standing, even when Russ gave him a nudge with his heels. Fooswah encouraged him to kick harder, and finally Outlaw started walking.

After a while Russ kicked him again, and Outlaw began to trot. Russ was mortified, when he bounced up and down. He pulled back on the reins. Outlaw stopped so suddenly, Russ nearly lost his seat.

Fooswah walked over, pressed his knee against the horse, and then clasped her hands together.

"Oh, I'm supposed to hold on with my knees," Russ said.

He tried again with more success. After an hour of riding, he decided to quit for the day. When he got off, his legs felt like rubber. Riding was hard work, but he'd practice every day until he got the hang of it.

Every morning after chores were completed, Russ rode Outlaw. He now could bridle and saddle the horse without help, but couldn't mount from the ground. A tree stump just the right height became his mounting aid. Fooswah no longer stayed outside with him, which made him feel much more confident.

They worked the garden spot every day, but hadn't planted anything yet. Russ realized that was changing when he noticed Fooswah gathering up containers of different seeds. Sure enough, early in the afternoon she used her hoe to make dirt mounds, spacing them about two feet apart. Russ tried, but his attempt failed to meet approval. Fooswah took his hoe. She picked up a can of corn kernels to be used for seed and demonstrated how to drop two in each mound.

"I've got it," Russ said and began dropping seeds.

After he placed the corn kernels, Fooswah showed him how to punch a hole alongside the corn and drop in two bean seeds. On the other side she planted squash. Through signs, she explained the corn growing tall and the beans growing up and around it.

Tulip tried to help, but was mostly in the way. Russ finally tied her to a tree limb in some nice green grass.

"You eat and quit bugging us," he told her.

She ate for a while. Then she untied herself and came back to help. Fooswah flapped her apron at Tulip. Instead of running away, the burro ran circles around Fooswah, messing up some of the mounds.

Russ captured the ornery critter and played chase with her back to the cabin. Together they mixed pig feed and carried it to the pen, only to find it empty.

"Dad-blamed pigs," he said to Tulip. "Let's go find them."

It didn't take long. The critters were in the garden with Fooswah yelling at them.

Russ ran back for the bucket of feed and then headed to the garden.

Fooswah was after them with a hoe, but the pigs thought it was a game. They ran, squealed, and made a mess of newly planted rows. Russ finally got their attention, enticed them to the pen, and fixed another hole.

By the time he finished, it was almost dark. He quickly fed Outlaw and Tulip. Once in the cabin, he noticed the empty water bucket. Away to the creek he went.

* * *

TULIP nudged Russ awake at first light. He fussed at her in a gentle tone, gave her a hug, and climbed from his bedroll on very sore legs.

Fooswah watched him hobble to the cabin.

After breakfast, she motioned for him to come with her. Russ followed her to the lean-to. Through her signs, he understood they were going to see Owen and get more seeds. Together they bridled and saddled Outlaw. She surprised him by mounting, riding next to a large stump, and indicating for him to climb on behind her.

Owen met them at the door and spoke to Fooswah in Creek. Three strange men hung around, looking at items but not buying anything.

One of the dirty, ugly men spotted Russ. "Hey look, a red-headed Indian kid. What do you fellows make of that?"

"I doubt he's Indian," one of the others answered. "Let's take him to Fort Sill. Maybe there's a reward for him."

Owen Hunter laid a .45 on the countertop. "You ain't taking him nowhere. Get gone from here."

A blond in filthy buckskins stood tall. "We ain't finished our business."

"You have five minutes," Owen replied.

The men bought a few items, mostly tobacco and ammunition, and then left. They gave Russ a long, hard look before heading out the door.

That night Fooswah, Russ, and Tulip all slept in the cabin with the shotgun close at hand. She even carried the gun to the garden with them. They remained tense and careful for several days.

Russ carried a water bucket to the creek and returned to the garden to water the mounds of seeds. He spilled a bit when Tulip brayed loud and long. Without hesitating, he took the bucket, called to the burro and ran to the cabin. Looking back, he saw someone riding through the trees along the creek. Fooswah met him at the door with the shotgun. They stayed near the cabin the rest of the day, keeping Tulip and the shotgun close.

"I sure wish Jeb would come riding in," Russ told Tulip. "He'd send those varmints packin'."

* * * * *

CHAPTER 16

TULIP didn't like being in the cabin, but Russ finally got her settled down beside his pallet.

Fooswah went to her bed. Russ noticed she didn't change into sleeping garments and simply stretched out on top of the covers. Nerves were tight and senses highly alert. Every strange sound caused a quickened heartbeat, a heightened awareness. Sleep was doubtful.

Despite intending to stay awake, Russ drifted off to sleep. Something disturbed him. He propped himself up on his elbow.

Tulip got to her feet and walked toward the door. She brayed just as the cabin door burst open.

"Watch that jackass," one of the men said.

Tulip rewarded him with a kick in the shin.

As the intruder hopped around, Russ whacked him with the fireplace poker. The man tried to get away from Tulip, but she wheeled and kicked him with both hind hooves. He stumbled out the doorway and collided with two other men, who were pushing to get inside the cabin.

They changed their minds, when Fooswah took a pot of hot water from the stove and threw it on them. Their cussing and howling changed to screams, when Tulip bared her teeth and ran out after them.

The surprised men ran for cover with a mad burro on their heels.

After chasing them to the edge of the timber, Tulip returned carrying a piece of material in her mouth.

Giving her a thorough inspection, Russ found no injuries. "You saved us, Tulip."

Fooswah made a fuss over her, too, and gave her a big piece of bread.

"I'm sorry I've brought trouble to you," Russ apologized.

She shook her head and smoothed back his hair. "No trouble."

Without a pause he wrapped his arms around her and hugged her. She returned his hug and then turned to the stove to cook an early breakfast.

When daylight arrived, Russ and Tulip left the cabin. They checked the lean-to and found Outlaw gone. The men also had taken the pigs. Russ ran to the cabin to alert Fooswah. She took off her apron, picked up the shotgun, and signaled for Russ to come with her.

"Maybe I should go to the post and get Owen," Russ said.

Fooswah shook her head and walked slowly around the area. When she found the men's tracks, she struck out in a trot. Russ ran beside her with Tulip bringing up the rear.

The thieves must not have worried about being caught, because they had camped only about three miles from the cabin.

Fooswah and Russ watched from behind a clump of bushes. While one man built a fire, another picked up the coffeepot and turned in the direction of the creek. Fooswah slipped away to follow him.

Russ trailed behind, careful to make no noise.

When the man squatted down to dip the pot in the stream, Fooswah snuck up behind him and rapped him over the head with the gun barrel. Russ helped her drag him into the woods, tie, and gag him.

Back they went just in time to save a pig. The blond-headed man held a knife to the little guy's throat, but changed his mind when Fooswah pulled back the hammer on the shotgun. He didn't offer any resistance, while Russ stood guard and Fooswah tied him hand and foot.

Tulip cornered the third man and began to bray. It was hard for Russ not to laugh at the situation. The outlaw stood in his long-johns with his trousers around his ankles, which made it difficult for him to do much maneuvering.

"Good job, Tulip," Russ said.

"Get that mule away from me, boy, or I'll shoot her."

"Don't think so. I've got your gun. You left it over by a stump."

"That gun's loaded. Put it down before you hurt somebody." The outlaw reached down to pull up his pants, but froze.

"You'd best be still," Russ said, pulling back the hammer on the pistol. "This gun might go off."

"Easy now. Don't do nothin' foolish. I'll stay right still."

Fooswah came to find them. With the shotgun leveled on him, the man was soon tied up. Russ collected weapons, put out the fire, packed their supplies, and decided to take their boots.

By early afternoon, they made their way back to the cabin. It must have been quite a sight. Three barefoot men with their hands tied behind their backs, two frolicking pigs, four horses, a feisty burro, an elderly woman, and a slender young boy.

After the pigs were secured and fed, Russ saddled Outlaw and led him to the cabin. All the while Fooswah stood guard over the prisoners. In a short time, she was mounted with the shotgun across her lap. Russ rode one of the outlaws' horses and carried a pistol. Tulip ran in circles around the captured men, letting them know she was ready for trouble.

It caused quite a stir at the trading post when Fooswah and Russ came in with three prisoners. The would-be kidnappers walked barefoot with their hands tied behind their backs. If one lagged, Tulip gave him a healthy head-butt from behind. People lined the way, chattering and laughing.

Owen Hunter roared with laughter, when he heard Fooswah's story. Picking up a length of new rope, he fashioned a hangman's noose and turned his gaze on the prisoners. "I told you three to git from here. Did you not hear me?"

"We'll git," one of the men said. "You'll never see us again."

"Tell you what. Some of my friends will ride along to Comanche Territory and let you go. How's that suit you?"

"Not good," the blond said, "but it's better than hanging."

"Strip their saddles," Owen ordered. "They can ride bareback. Hang on to their weapons, until you turn them loose."

If the outlaws disagreed, they kept it to themselves.

"Fooswah tracked those outlaws right to their camp," Russ said, as he snuck a cracker for Tulip. "Of course, the pigs squealing kinda gave away their location."

"What about when they broke into the cabin?" Owen asked. "How did you stop them?"

"I hit one with the poker. Fooswah threw hot water on them. And Tulip went to work with her teeth." Russ gave a big grin. "They couldn't get out the door fast enough."

"Good work," Owen said, chuckling.

The three outlaws accompanied by five braves left the post bootless and riding bareback. Once they were out of sight, Russ breathed a sigh of relief. Fooswah smiled at him and started for the door.

Riding double with their faithful, cracker-stuffed burro following, they made their way home.

Russ took Outlaw to the lean-to, rubbed him down, and fed both him and Tulip. Exhausted, he managed to finish his chores, feeding the pigs and fetching water. Finally, he washed up and sat down at the table. Before Fooswah got supper served, he fell asleep.

The next morning he awoke on a pallet. He didn't remember Fooswah removing his boots, but he did remember his dream. In it Jeb had ridden in with a pretty pinto pony and said: "He's all yours."

* * * * *

CHAPTER 17

RUSS ran to the lean-to expecting to see a beautiful, pinto pony. As usual, it was just Tulip and Outlaw.

In anguish, he wrapped his arms around Tulip and cried. Perhaps it was the disappointment of realizing he had only dreamed of the pony or it let-down from yesterday's excitement. In his moment of despair, he longed for his mother's arms and his father's voice.

The little burro didn't move one step, while his friend grieved.

As suddenly as it had started, the crying stopped.

"I bet the water bucket's empty."

Later at the breakfast table Fooswah gave him a puzzled look and then went about her daily chores. For lunch she fixed the little honey-covered cornmeal cakes that Russ loved.

As they worked that afternoon in the garden, Osekee came running in jabbering. He was going hunting and wanted Russ to go with him.

Russ turned to Fooswah. "Can I go hunting with Osekee?"

She nodded and smiled.

"Come on, while I get my bow and arrows," Russ said to Osekee.

The two boys rushed to the cabin, where Russ picked up his hunting equipment. Suddenly, his world was bright again.

Osekee didn't want Tulip to go with them, convinced she would scare off any game.

Russ left his friend in the lean-to, after he explained to her this was an important mission.

They headed for the river hoping to find a turkey, deer, or a rabbit. Anything edible was in danger from such mighty hunters. Osekee found the track of a buck. In broken English, he explained a buck track had two indentions at the back of the hoofprint, which a doe didn't have. From the size of the track, it was a big buck. In their excitement, the boys paid no attention to the direction they headed. In and out of the trees, vines, and bushes they weaved, heads down, eyes on the vivid tracks.

The buck had crossed a fast-running creek. The boys were reluctant to follow, but Osekee found a place where the creek narrowed with several large rocks just above the surface of the water.

Ignoring the danger, Osekee jumped from rock to rock.

Russ followed, but at one point he slipped off a rock and slid into the water. Wet, he scrambled back up and on across.

Time got away from them, and it was late in the afternoon.

Russ grew tired of the discomfort of wet britches. "Let's go back."

Osekee agreed.

Again they crossed the creek. They backtracked the buck for a while, and then discovered the trail destroyed by the hooves of several cattle. Assuming they were going in the right direction, they trudged onward.

Daylight began to fade. The two hunters were lost, cold, and hungry. Osekee started gathering sticks. Using his knife, he cut a hole in a flat piece of dry wood. He unstrung his bow and wrapped the string around a smooth, straight stick and restrung it. One end of the stick he placed in the hole. Osekee held the bow parallel to the ground and began pulling it back and forward causing the stick to rotate.

Russ stood by with dead grass to place on the wood once it started to smoke. It looked easy when one of the braves started a fire using the twirling stick method, but after fifteen minutes of hard work, there wasn't even a spark. Both boys were discouraged, but a curl of smoke boosted their efforts and at last a flame appeared. Careful not to add too much fuel at a time they soon had a nice fire.

As night birds called, small critters scurried about and coyotes howled. The light and warmth of the fire was a comfort, but hunger ate at their stomachs. Fear crept in, and the warriors weren't so brave.

"Boy, I'm hungry," Russ said rubbing his stomach.

Osekee nodded in agreement.

Russ sat with his head lowered to his pulled-up knees. "I will not cry. I will not cry," he told himself. A single tear slid down his cheek. He slipped his hand under his leg and wiped away the tear. Then he peeked to see if Osekee had noticed. His friend was asleep, so that meant Russ must keep the fire going. That was okay. He was cold, scared, and not the least bit sleepy, or so he thought until something bumped into him.

He jerked awake, not realizing he had fallen asleep. Terrified Russ jumped to his feet and cried out. A soft voice calmed him, and Tulip rubbed against him.

Relieved, he hugged the burro. "How did you find us?"

Fooswah pointed to Tulip.

Perhaps even better than being found was the food Fooswah brought with her. She also had a couple of blankets Tulip had toted for her. It was hard to tell which was better, a warm blanket or beef jerky and a biscuit.

Tulip lay beside her friend.

"I'll never leave you at home again," Russ whispered, before he drifted into peaceful slumber.

Fooswah woke the hunters early the next morning. They followed her through vines and stickers to get back to the main trail. Russ was amazed when he realized they had gotten lost so close to home.

Osekee took off after breakfast. Russ wished for more sleep, but grabbed the water bucket and headed for the creek. The pigs greeted him with squeals and grunts.

"I'll feed you guys in a little bit," he assured them.

He finished his chores and planned to ride Outlaw. His plans changed when Fooswah came from the cabin and called to him. She indicated that he should come with her. Together they walked to the woods across the creek from the cabin. On the way she pointed out landmarks that Russ hadn't noticed. A large rock, a tall cottonwood, and a big plum thicket were all easily recognized.

She showed him how to tell directions from moss on trees and from where the sun sat in the sky. All of these things she explained without saying a word. Russ was amazed at how much the little woman knew about the wild. He was more amazed when she removed a piece of rock and something else from the bag she always wore around her neck. Using the rock, some kind of metal, a bit of cloth, and some dry grass, she started a fire. Then she handed him the flint and steel, so he could try. It took him a while, but he finally succeeded.

They spent most of the day in the woods. When it began to get late in the afternoon, Fooswah took a piece of cloth from around her neck, blindfolded Russ with it, and turned him in a circle. When he recovered from being dizzy and removed the blindfold, Fooswah and Tulip were gone. Panic was his first reaction. Then he took in his surroundings and began using his newly acquired knowledge.

At first it was easy. He followed her footprints and Tulip's hoofprints. Feeling quite smug, he whistled as he went. Suddenly, there were no prints. He circled the area and noticed a broken stick and part of a print. Carefully, he searched and found their trail. Three times he lost them, but managed to find their direction.

Fooswah stepped out in front of him, startling him. She laughed, as together they crossed the creek to the cabin.

The next day after chores were done, Fooswah took a stick and drew a map in the dirt yard. On one side of the map was the river with various creeks branching out from it. Directly to the south of a large bend in the river was where the cabin was located. The trading post was further on and south of the cabin with a scattering of dwellings about.

That afternoon they walked away from the cabin, only this time Russ walked blindfolded. He tried to estimate how far they went, but couldn't tell. Again, Fooswah spun him around and left.

Tulip brayed, as if to say good luck.

Picturing the map in his head, Russ decided to head to the river and find the big bend. He listened, but couldn't hear running water. Slowly, he turned in a circle, but didn't recognize any landmarks. There was a pretty tall hill not far away, so he walked to it and climbed to the top. There was still no river in sight, but off to his left was a tall cottonwood. It was possible there was more than one such tree, but this one was really tall. He was in luck. This was the tree near the cabin.

There were more lessons on directions, tracking, and landmarks. Russ absorbed information like a sponge and soon could almost beat Fooswah back home. In addition to their lessons, they worked the garden and cared for the animals.

The day Fooswah took him out in the evening and left him was scary, but he felt sure he could find his way home. After a day and a night in the woods, he began to doubt his abilities. He remembered Jeb saying *follow a river, and it will take you somewhere*. Russ could hear running water. He hoped it was the right river. Late that afternoon, he found the bend that Fooswah had drawn on the map. The cabin lay just south from where he stood.

Tulip and Fooswah were headed away from the cabin, when Russ came walking up the trail. Tulip brayed a greeting, and Fooswah gave a big smile.

Now if Jeb needs to find an outlaw, Russ thought as they walked toward home, *I can help track him.*

* * * * *

Part IV

Burris

CHAPTER 18

JEB pushed his borrowed mount hard.

He reached Fort Sill just before dark. After filling in the officer in charge about Captain Webster, Jeb put his weary horse in a pen for the night and checked on Brownie. Three days of rest showed his friend to be in good shape.

"Well, old buddy, good times are over," he said with a sigh. "We've a long trip ahead of us."

Sunrise brought the promise of a beautiful day. Jeb rode south from Fort Sill with Fort Worth in mind. With no delays he should make it in three days, but all manner of things could happen during that time of year. Indians prowled, looking for meat and unsuspecting folks. The trail herds on the move were another favorite target.

Jeb made a cattle drive when he was fifteen. His uncle signed him on as the remuda wrangler. His job was controlling a large herd of horses. Thankfully, some of the older hands helped him. It had been a long trip from Texas to Wyoming, suffering all kinds of weather, river crossings, cattle thieves, stampedes, and Indian attacks. Jeb survived, but his uncle didn't. His uncle's horse went down in a rush of frightened cattle. They buried what was left of him in northern New Mexico.

A blur of movement ahead caught Jeb's attention. He rode cautiously and soon met a couple of cowboys.

"Howdy," said a tall and lean young man.

"Howdy. Where you fellas headed?"

"Our boss back at the Double T sent us out to check the grass. He's chomping at the bit to head to Kansas with a herd."

"Won't be long if the weather holds," Jeb offered. "Did you happen to hear of any Indian trouble down your way? I'm looking for a murdering half-breed who's running with at least two Indian braves."

"Ain't seen nobody, Indian or white, since we crossed the Red. Before the crossing, we ran into a couple of settlers."

"Have any trouble crossing the river?

The tall young man shook his head. "No, it's pretty shallow right now. Just watch for quicksand."

"You boys keep a sharp eye," Jeb suggested. "Be sure and take extra underwear when you make the drive."

"Why underwear?" the short stocky cowboy asked.

"You'll figure it out after the first stampede."

The cowboys laughed and wished Jeb luck with his search.

At dusk Jeb looked for a suitable place to camp. For some reason he felt uncomfortable, like someone or something was watching him. When the sun went down, he fixed his bed, put his hat on the saddle he used for a pillow, and slipped into the woods. He heard someone approaching his bedroll. The click of a pistol hammer caught his attention.

"Drop it," Jeb said before a shot was fired, "or I'll blow you away."

"Easy man. I wasn't going to shoot."

"Get down on your knees and put your hands on your head."

The stranger did as instructed. Jeb wished for some light. He couldn't be sure the man was unarmed. To be safe, he tossed a limb off to one side. Sure, enough the guy shot.

"You missed, and I'm thinking about killing you."

Jeb heard the gun hit the ground.

"I ain't gonna try nothing else," the man vowed.

"You'd best behave. I'm not in the mood to mess with you."

Jeb tied the visitor to a tree, crawled into his bedroll, and slept soundly until daylight.

The man who shot at him was a pitiful sight, dirty and skinny with a long beard and greasy long hair.

"When's the last time you ate?" Jeb asked.

"Been a few days. I had a deer in my sights, but an Indian beat me to it. I was afeared to hang around, so I traveled on. Seemed like every time I found some game an Indian or two showed up."

"Where you headed?"

"No place. Just looking over the country."

Jeb built a fire, cooked breakfast, and fed the man all he could eat. He put away a good portion of vittles.

When Jeb saw his horse, he knew what the guy was after. Poor creature was thin and sway-backed. If possible, he looked worse than his owner.

"I'm taking your guns, but will leave them by that big cottonwood. You'd best go on about your way and leave me alone. I'd hate to shoot you, but I will."

"I surely ain't gonna' bother you. Thank ye for the food. I won't be forgetting that."

Sunrise came and was beautiful. Every body of water, large or small had steam rising from it, giving the land a mysterious look. The world was alive with bird calls and animals scampering across the open areas.

A long line of fog told Jeb he was near the Red River. He would ask questions at the trading post. Maybe someone knew something about Burris. As he pondered the best route, it occurred to him that it might be easier to learn more out about the Indian woman and the little boy. Surely, someone knew of them.

He found no answers at the trading post, but restocked his supplies, ate a filling meal, fed Brownie, and crossed the river. The river was shallow like the cowboys had said, but full of snags and quicksand.

Jeb reached Fort Worth late in the afternoon and headed straight for the Tumbleweed Saloon to get the latest news. There were several horses tied to the hitching rail. Jeb tied Brownie alongside them.

Using his hat, he slapped dust from his shirt and pants before entering the bat-wing doors. He stood for a minute to let his eyes adjust to the dark interior. Then he walked to the bar and ordered rye, although he didn't really like to drink.

The bartender was a short and stocky man who was friendly but didn't have any answers about the woman and child. "Hey Oscar!" he hollered across the room to a man sitting with a group playing poker. "You know anything about a squaw with a kid in these parts?"

"Heard of such a woman over west of here," Oscar replied, "but that's been a while back. You might check with the sheriff."

The sheriff's office was easy to find, but the lawman was gone. Jeb talked to several folks up and down the street, but no one could tell him about a disfigured Indian woman with a young son. Maybe he had made a mistake not looking for Burris. He'd give it a couple of days, and if he didn't find out anything he would backtrack.

Weary, he rode to the livery and paid to stable Brownie. Once his mount was rubbed down good and had a bait of corn, Jeb walked to the mercantile. He bought a new suit of clothes, which he donned after a bath and a shave.

Feeling like a new man, he walked into Mama's Cafe for a good meal. Minutes later he was enjoying a heaping plate of steak, mashed potatoes, gravy, and many cups of hot coffee.

A tall, thin man sporting a handle-bar mustache and a star on his shirt walked over to his table. "Buck Jones," the man said. "I hear you're seeking information."

"Howdy, Sheriff." Jeb nodded to a chair. "My name's Jebediah Powers. I'm a Texas Ranger looking for a half-breed named Henry Burris."

"I've heard of Burris. What makes you think he's in these parts?"

"Story is he's helping a Comanche brave find his son. Evidently, the brave was messing with a young woman the chief had his eye on. When the chief found out, he cut off part of her nose and kicked her out. Don't know how the brave knew she was with child, but now he wants his kid."

"I've heard of such a woman. She was taken in by some people who live over between the Trinity and the Brazos. Let's go talk with Dr. Alexander. He's been out there."

The doctor wasn't in his office. Jeb and the sheriff looked around town for him. Ike Jones at the post office said he had gone to the Robinson place to deliver a baby.

Getting general directions from the sheriff, Jeb decided to ride out on his own the next morning.

Green grass sparkled with dew, as Jeb and Brownie left Fort Worth. It was a pleasant morning, and Jeb rode hoping to find the Indian woman and get some information. This seemed to be a popular route, although most people were going toward Fort Worth, not in his direction.

Travelers thinned out as he rode farther from town. It would probably take another day to get near where he needed to go, so he bought extra grub in Fort Worth. He camped along a small creek, ate, and slept well.

A lovely spring day greeted him. He rode alert, but not really expecting trouble. That proved to be a mistake.

Early that afternoon Jeb rode down a creek bank thinking about a cool drink of water for himself and Brownie. An arrow hit him in his right thigh. Despite the pain he put spurs to Brownie to get out of range. Blood ran down his leg into his boot. Struggling to hold onto the reins, he pulled his pistol and fired a shot at a disappearing Indian. A second arrow hit him in the back. Then he was slipping out of the saddle.

His last thoughts before darkness took him were of a little boy who waited for him and of Lillian who could never be his.

* * * * *

CHAPTER 19

PAIN plagued Jeb to the point he feared he might scream.

Instead, he moaned and tried to find an escape from it. He was aware of moving in some type of wagon, but couldn't recall what put him there. When he thought he had a grip on things, the pain took control. Jeb didn't really care where he was. He just wanted some relief.

His mind drifted from one foggy thought to another. A soft hand reminded him of a kind, black woman from his childhood. When reality returned, he knew it had been just a pain induced dream.

A familiar voice, but who spoke? A child's laughter. Confusion beset him, as he struggled to escape the agony that possessed him.

He had no sense of day or night or of his surroundings. Death was almost wished for, but he remembered a promise he had made.

A kind hand touched his face with a cool rag, an unusual experience for the Texas Ranger. He opened his eyes to find a woman tending to him.

"Well, hello," she said in a pleasant voice.

He tried to sit up, but a stab of pain changed his plan. "Where am I?"

"I think you know my husband, Bart. I'm Nancy Jamison, and you are a guest in our home."

Jeb nodded and tried to smile. "Where is he?"

"He's doing chores, but will be in for supper soon. You rest. I'll bring you some broth."

Nancy fed Jeb only a few spoons of the warm soup before he tired and drifted into sleep. He slept fitfully and never free of pain.

A strange voice got his attention.

"Give him a spoonful of this every four hours to help the pain. I'm not worried about his leg, but the back wound could be serious.

"Mr. Powers, I'm Doctor Alexander. I'm going to give you something to help your pain. Then examine your wounds. Do you think you can handle being moved around a bit?"

Jeb nodded and opened his mouth. The medicine he swallowed was bitter and tasted awful. After a while, the pain became more bearable. Not gone, but less intense.

"Getting a little relief?" Dr. Alexander asked.

"A bit," Jeb replied.

"I'm going to see what we need to do to get you well. This may hurt some."

The doctor didn't lie. Jeb about came unglued when he was rolled onto his side. After poking and prodding his back wound for what seemed like an hour, the doctor eased him flat on the bed.

Jeb had a strong urge to punch the man, but remembered the medicine. Before he made any comment or batted an eye, the doctor spooned more of the bitter concoction into his mouth.

"Thought you might need a little extra about now."

Jeb hurt too much to say thanks. He did manage to nod.

"The wound in your back is serious. I think the arrow hit your kidney. I want to put in a tube to drain the excess blood. Once the bleeding stops, it should heal. I don't want to operate unless it's absolutely necessary. Is my plan okay with you?"

"I'll go along with whatever you say, Doc. What about my leg?"

"Your leg is going to be fine. Sparrow took care of it for you."

"Who's Sparrow?"

"She's a Comanche woman who lives near Bart and Nancy."

"Does she have a disfigured nose and a little boy?"

"Why, yes she does. How did you know that?"

"I came this direction to find her," Jeb replied. "She's in danger and so is the boy."

"What do you mean? What kind of danger?"

"The boy's father is coming for him."

"Oh, lord. I'd best let Bart know. And Sparrow."

"I think there's at least three braves headed this way. Well, two braves and a half-breed outlaw named Burris. I'm inclined to think they're the ones that shot me."

"I'll talk to Bart," Doctor Alexander said from the doorway. "Then come back and put in the tube."

"What you need to talk to me about?" a tall, handsome man asked.

"I'll let Mr. Powers tell you," the doctor answered.

"Hello, old friend." Bart stuck a large hand Jeb's way.

Jeb took his hand. "Hello. Thanks for taking me in."

"I'll put you to work, as soon as you're able. What brings you to these parts?"

"I chased a sorry half-breed all the way to the North Canadian River in Indian Territory, only to have him get away from me. Somewhere along the line he joined up with a couple of Comanche braves who were headed to Texas to look for a woman and a child. The woman was kicked out of her tribe for messing with the brave. He got word that she was with child when she left. He decided he had a son and now wants him."

Bart turned for the door. "I've got to get Sparrow and Hoot and bring them here. I'll be back in a while, Jeb. You rest easy."

Doctor Alexander returned with all sorts of equipment. "I'm going to give you ether and put a drain tube in your back, which means you'll have to lie on your side or stomach. I doubt the tube will have to stay in long. Do you have any questions?"

"If the arrow did hit my kidney, will it be okay?"

"I think the arrow went deep enough to puncture your kidney and was further irritated when you were moved. With time and rest the kidney will heal. I'm going to leave a bottle of laudanum for you. Take it sparingly. The stuff is addictive. Ready to take a nap?"

"I reckon," Jeb mumbled.

"Nancy," Doctor Alexander called from the doorway. "Can you come administer the ether for me?"

"I'll be right there," the pert, little woman answered.

"We'll put him to sleep on his back. Then turn him onto his side or stomach. Put that mask over his nose and mouth. When I tell you, put a drop or two of this liquid onto the mask. It shouldn't take much to knock him out. You may have to add more if he starts coming around. I'll try to be quick."

"Jeb, you're in good hands," Nancy said. "Doctor Alexander is a highly skilled man."

"Good. Let's get it done."

The tube was inserted, stitched in place, and hung so it drained into a large jar. By the time Jeb woke up Doctor Alexander was gone.

Jeb felt awful from the aftereffects of ether. His head ached, his thoughts swarmed like a hive of bees, and his back hurt like hell.

"How are you feeling?" Nancy asked.

"Not so good. I think I'm going to puke." When he started gagging, Nancy held a pan for him. He heaved a couple of times, but nothing came up. "Sorry, I'm such a bother."

"You're no bother," Nancy assured him.

Bart came into the room and sat down in a chair next to Jeb's bed. "How you doing?'

"Not so hot right now. I feel like I did when I got drunk on rot-gut whiskey. Did you warn the woman?"

"I brought her home with me. We'll keep her here to make sure she's safe. Tell me what you know about these Indians and this Burris guy."

Jeb started to tell Bart about chasing Burris, but couldn't keep his eyes open.

As he drifted off to sleep, his last thoughts were about the little boy Russ and the possibility that Fooswah could be Bart's aunt.

* * * * *

CHAPTER 20

DAYS passed through a haze of pain and drug-induced stupor.

Jeb struggled to understand his situation. For five days Nancy, Bart, and Sparrow sponged him with cool water to help keep down his fever.

Dr. Alexander returned and examined Jeb's wounds. The one in his back had quit bleeding, so he removed the tube.

The big danger now was infection, which was likely the cause of the fever. It was a case of how much fight Jeb had in him.

When his fever broke, Jeb couldn't hold up his head. Bart sponged the sweat from his friend's body. Then lifted him from the bed, while Nancy changed the linens. He ate a few spoons of broth and slowly fell into deep sleep.

Jeb soon began to improve. The day finally came when he was strong enough to talk. "Bart, I believe Burris is headed this way and might be the one who shot me. He's with a couple of braves. One of them thinks a Comanche woman lives in these parts and has his son. He's determined to get the boy."

"Yes, we know. You told us already. The woman is called Sparrow. She and the boy are here with us."

"Has there been any trouble?"

"Not any direct attack," Bart said, "but I'm missing a cow, and my neighbor had a couple of horses stolen. We're keeping a sharp eye out."

Their conversation was interrupted by a small, dark-haired whirlwind who came running into the room.

"Sam, slow down," Bart ordered.

In a flash, the little boy jumped onto his father's lap and stared at Jeb.

"Howdy." Jeb smiled at the youngster and held out his hand. "My name's Jeb. What's yours?"

"I'm Sam. You get up."

"Well, I'm hoping to get up and about first thing tomorrow. Maybe you can show me around the place."

"Okay." Sam jumped to the floor and raced out of the room.

"Handsome boy," Jeb said.

"I'm just glad he wasn't twins. It takes all of us to keep up with him."

"Did you get Chief Many Horses back to his tribe?" Jeb asked.

"Yes," Bart replied. "He kept his word and let me and Katie leave. Even gave her a pony. We caught some trouble after we crossed the Red. Nancy's husband and a couple of his buddies robbed the trading post and were high-tailing it out of the area. We ran into them. Bob, Nancy's husband, shot me. Katie snuck me a gun and got away on Ace. One of the guys went after her. The other two got to fighting about their situation. Bob shot his partner. Then came to finish me off, so I shot him."

"Dang. Sounds like you had plenty of trouble. How'd Nancy take you killing her husband?"

"I think she was relieved," Bart said. "He was no account. Forced her to go with him, so she could cook. Was mean to his son. Just all around no good. I was sure she'd run me off, but instead she married me."

"Sounds like you did her a favor. Can you help me stand up for a minute? I need to start working on getting my strength back. Sam's right. I've been in bed a lot."

Jeb stood for maybe a minute before he broke out in a cold sweat and became lightheaded. "Best sit me down, Bart. I feel a little weak-kneed."

Back in bed with a dose of laudanum, Jeb drifted off to sleep.

For several days, Bart helped him out of bed. The day finally came when Jeb could get up by himself and walk to the kitchen table.

It was a treat to join Nancy, Katie, Nancy's son Toby, Sam, and the Indian woman called Sparrow. Sparrow's son Hoot was standoffish, but Jeb thought he might warm up to him in time.

Jeb couldn't understand why Burris and his friends hadn't showed up. Maybe they had moved on or somebody had shot them. He'd do some scouting around in a day or two. His leg was about healed, but his back was mighty touchy. Riding didn't appeal to him, but he'd get back in the saddle, pain or no pain. Besides, Brownie needed some exercise.

He walked to the barn one fine spring morning with plans to ride around a bit. Katie, Toby, and Hoot were working colts in a round pen. All three kids were excellent with horses, but Katie outshined the boys. Jeb admired the beautiful horseflesh. Bart's plan to breed and train top-notch horses looked to be panning out.

He picked up Brownie's bridle and whistled. The horse came racing from the pasture.

As Jeb picked up his saddle, Bart rode over and swung from his horse.

"Hold it, Jeb. Let me do that for you. No need to start those wounds bleeding again."

"I'm obliged," Jeb said.

"Let's see if we pick up any signs of trouble." Bart gestured to the colt he was riding. "I need to get some miles on this young'un."

They left the barn lot and were headed into open country just as a big man came riding toward them.

"That's my friend, Daniel," Bart said. "He's the one that found you."

Greetings were exchanged.

"Someone was in Sparrow's cabin last night or this morning." Daniel said. "I've checked it every day, and this is the first sign I've seen."

"Was one of them riding a pigeon-toed horse?" Jeb asked.

"Sure was. How'd you know that?"

"I've been tracking him from Indian Territory," Jeb explained. "How many of them you think?"

"Three or maybe four," Daniel replied.

Bart turned his mount in the direction of Sparrow's cabin. "Let's go have a look."

They approached the area with caution.

Sure enough, Jeb spotted familiar hoof-prints.

Bart checked the cabin and didn't think anything was missing. He insisted Jeb return to the ranch. Jeb protested, but reined Brownie back the way they'd come.

"Keep a sharp eye out," Jeb advised. "These guys are killers."

"Guard my place for me," Bart said.

Jeb thought he'd never get back. Waves of pain made it hard to breathe. Finally, the corrals came into view. He decided to take a turn along the timberline bordering the pasture. Pain was forgotten when he spotted fresh tracks in the soft ground. Without hesitation he kicked Brownie into a lope and headed toward the cabin.

I owe you, Burris. I intend to pay you for all you've done, especially for killing a little boy's ma and pa.

Katie was milking, while Hoot mucked out stalls.

Toby, who was in the barn feeding horses, dropped the feed bucket and ran to help unsaddle Brownie. "You look done in. I'll take care of your horse."

"Thank you, son. I've about had it. Think I'll rest on the porch a spell." Jeb took his rifle from its boot and made his way to the cabin. He really wanted to collapse on the bed, but a hard-backed chair would have to do for now.

Nancy came out to check on him and insisted he go inside.

"I need to watch for Burris and his cronies," Jeb protested.

"I'll stand guard," Nancy informed him.

Before Jeb went into the cabin, Nancy stationed Toby in the barn loft, Hoot in the pecan tree, and Katie inside the house watching out the back window. It was doubtful a mouse could get past those youngsters.

The weary ranger stretched out on the bed and closed his eyes.

"Toby spotted some riders west of here!" Nancy hollered. "Riding this way!"

* * * * *

CHAPTER 21

AT Nancy's call, Jeb scrambled out of bed.

He jammed the hat on his head, stomped into his boots, strapped on his pistol, and joined Nancy on the porch. "Where were they when you spotted them?"

"Just this side of the timberline to the north. See that big cottonwood? They were almost directly under it."

"How many?"

"Four, I think."

"I have a spyglass in my saddlebag," Jeb said.

"Stay put. I'll get it."

Jeb feared that bunch might try to lure people out of the house by stampeding the horses. "Can you get the horses to the barn?"

"Toby!" Nancy hollered. "Whistle in Ace and the mares!"

A shrill whistle brought the horses running. In a few minutes, they were in the corral near the barn.

Toby made sure the gate was tied, and then went back to his post in the hay loft. "They're moving back into the timber!"

"What do you think they'll do now?" Nancy asked Jeb.

"I'm not sure. I'd feel better, if we could warn Bart. They've probably been scouting the place for a spell and know how many are here."

"Do you think they'll attack us?"

"Don't know, but we'd best be ready. Can the young'uns shoot?"

"Yes. I'll call them in one at a time and give them a rifle," Nancy said as she turned to go get weapons. "Or should I arm them with shotguns?"

"It would be best to discourage them with rifles. Don't want them in shotgun range if we can help it."

"I'm worried about Bart." Nancy carefully loaded a Henry rifle. "He's apt to ride right into them."

"I'll fire a couple of rounds to let him know something's going on." Jeb stepped off the porch, raised his pistol, and shot into the air.

With sunset near Jeb was also concerned about Bart. If it wasn't for the women and children, he would saddle up and look for him.

Nancy called Jeb to supper, but he told her he'd best stay where he could keep an eye on things. She brought him a plate and a cup of coffee. In a minute she took a plate to Toby. On her return, she stopped under the pecan tree and told Hoot to come eat.

Daylight was fading fast.

"Horse coming in at a run!" Toby hollered.

Jeb left the porch in a rush, causing a stab of pain in his back. "Damn." It came out of his mouth before he knew it. He'd best be more careful, because one small boy would be repeating him.

Toby came from the loft to open the gate for the colt Bart had been riding that morning. The young horse was lathered up and agitated, but didn't have any wounds.

"I'd better go look for Bart," Toby said. "I don't know a better rider than him. Something's happened."

"We have to hope it was a freak thing, and he's okay," Jeb said. "It's too dangerous for you to go alone."

The two stood looking into the distance, hoping to see Bart walking their way. When darkness fell Toby returned to the barn-loft and Jeb to the porch. Hoot remained in the pecan tree. The women and Sam were secure in the cabin.

Jeb felt tension in the air. He sat in a dark corner of the porch, alert and watchful. Despite the cool of the evening, he was sweating.

He listened for the usual night sounds: critters scurrying about, birds winging in to roost, an occasional hoot from an owl. There were no sounds, and that made him more nervous. He stood, moved closer to the cabin door, and froze in his tracks. There was someone on the roof. Not sure what to do, Jeb remained where he was.

Soft footsteps moved across the porch roof in the direction of the pecan tree. Jeb sensed the intruder was after Hoot. He slipped to the edge of the porch and waited. Just as the Indian jumped from the roof, Jeb threw him to the ground. Before he could subdue him, the brave was gone.

Hoot dropped from the tree to the ground. "You hurt?"

"Just my pride. I let him get away."

Together Hoot and Jeb walked to the cabin.

Sparrow was horrified when she learned what happened.

"Do you think they'll try anything again tonight?" Nancy asked.

"Not likely," Jeb answered. "They know we're watching for them."

"I'm going to look for Mister Bart," Katie announced.

Jeb shook his head. "No. It's too dangerous."

"I'll ride Ace, and he'll find Mister Bart. Nobody can get close if I'm on Ace. You have to stay here and protect the others, because this is where the trouble will be." Without another word she marched out the door.

"I won't be able to live with myself, if something happens to that girl," Jeb admitted.

Nancy poured Jeb a cup of coffee. "There was no stopping her, so don't beat yourself up."

Hoot stuck his head through the doorway. "Going to barn to stay with Toby."

"Spell each other off, so you can get some sleep," Jeb cautioned. "We'll handle things here. Keep an eye on the horses and be mighty careful."

Nancy stood guard, while Sparrow and Jeb slept.

Far into the night a coyote yipped. Or was it a coyote? Something about that yip didn't sound right. Jeb splashed water on his face, jammed on his hat, checked his pistol, and headed out the door.

"I'm going to check on the boys," he told Nancy.

He found them okay. Toby was asleep, while Hoot kept watch. Jeb walked to look out the opening that allowed hay to be hoisted into the loft. He knew something was wrong. The horses stood with ears perked toward the east. This time of night they should be relaxed.

"Hoot, hand me your rifle." Jeb jacked a shell into the chamber. "Tell your mother and Nancy to get ready. I think trouble's coming."

"Open the gate!" Katie yelled.

After waking Toby, Jeb climbed down the ladder and ran toward the gate. Katie raced his way with four or five Indians after her. Jeb opened fire at the braves, causing them to scatter in different directions.

"Keep your eye on them, Toby. Holler if they head this way again."

Somehow that young girl had not only found Bart, but had gotten onto Ace and held Bart in the saddle while being chased by Indians.

"Leave him in the saddle and lead Ace to the house."

"Has he been shot?" Nancy asked.

"No, I think he got pitched and hit his head on something. He came to long enough to help me get him into the saddle."

Jeb, Nancy, and Katie got Bart inside the cabin.

"Here they come!" Toby hollered. "Looks like five or six of them!"

* * * * *

CHAPTER 22

"TOBY, keep your eyes peeled and let us know what they're doing," Jeb ordered. "The rest of you gather. And bring buckets."

No one needed to ask what the buckets were for. They went to the well and filled them. Then they returned to Jeb.

"Okay, Toby has the barn covered. Katie, can you get on the roof and cover the back of the cabin?"

"You bet," was all Jeb heard as she scurried away.

"Hoot, you have the south side of the cabin. I'll take the west. Nancy's got the east. I think they'll spread out and start circling us. Don't shoot until they are in range and don't be disappointed if you don't hit anything. They'll drop off to one side of their horses. All we'll see is a leg and maybe an arm."

"How are we going to beat them, if we can't shoot them?" Nancy asked.

"Patience. Wait long enough, and they'll mess up. If this was in the middle of nowhere, they'd devil us into doing something stupid. Here they know there's a chance someone might happen by."

As everyone got into position, Bart walked out of the door. "Where do you want me?"

"Didn't know you was among the living." Jeb handed Bart a rifle. "Are you okay? Katie said you got a bump on the head."

"I'm fine. Just a little headache. The young'un didn't like a covey of quail under him."

"Take my spot. I'll try to get into the woods and come up behind them. Just don't shoot me by mistake."

Sam came flying out of the cabin, looking for his mother.

Bart caught him. "Stay with Sparrow. Understand?"

With tears rolling, Sam nodded and went to Sparrow. She took his hand, and together they went back inside the cabin.

Jeb slipped to the pecan tree and then to the chicken house. When one of the chickens squawked, he jumped and imagined the point of an arrow in his back. Chiding himself, he studied the best way to get to the barn. There was no cover. Since he couldn't run, he had no choice but to walk across and hope. With a sigh he made it to the barn unharmed.

"Toby, they still out there?"

"Two of 'em are. The others went into the woods along the creek."

Jeb's next objective was to reach the woods north of the barn. Maybe he could hide there and get the Indians sandwiched between him and the cabin. If the Indians had worked their way to the place he was headed, he was in big trouble.

He made it to the woods and listened. Nothing stirred, which was not a good sign. He slipped around a big cottonwood and hugged the rough bark of a hackberry. For several tense minutes he waited and listened. It was too quiet. Something wasn't right.

Then it hit him, the smell of woodsmoke and grease.

There was an Indian close, probably on the other side of the tree. Jeb knew he was in trouble. Shooting the man would bring the whole bunch down on him. He hadn't fully recovered from his wounds, so hand-to-hand combat favored the brave.

Before he could decide what to do, gunfire erupted near the cabin. Jeb stayed put, hoping the Indian would move first.

Bingo. The man on the other side of the hackberry took a step toward the cabin. Jeb slipped from behind the tree and clobbered him with the butt of his pistol, knocking him out cold. He tied his hands and feet and left him at the base of the hackberry.

One down, several to go, and he had no idea where they were. With sweat covering him, Jeb crept through the underbrush, alert to sounds and watchful for movement. Nothing.

"They're going to rush us!" Toby yelled from the barn.

Sure enough, they came at a mad run. Jeb stepped to the edge of the timber, hoping to get a shot or two. No such luck.

The Indians made a dash around the cabin and shot flaming arrows at the roof. A volley of gunfire discouraged them, and a bucket of water put out the fire. Away they went, yipping and screeching.

"Stay put!" Jeb ordered. "They may be back."

Night changed to day, and there were no more attacks. Jeb and Bart went to get the captured Indian, but he had gotten loose and escaped.

"That's twice someone has gotten away from me," Jeb grumbled. "Next time I'll just shoot him."

"No, you won't," Bart said. "You're too civilized for cold-blooded murder."

"I'm tired of this chasing game. After I catch Burris, I'm leaving the Rangers."

"What are you going to do?'

"Don't know for certain. First, I'm going back to get Russ and Tulip. Then decide from there."

The two men headed back to the cabin.

"Here they come!" Katie hollered.

The Indians caught Jeb and Bart between the woods and the cabin. Jeb knew he couldn't run and also knew Bart wouldn't leave him.

"Hunker down with your back to mine. We'll make them wish they'd picked on somebody else." Jeb squatted low to the ground. "Got plenty of ammo?"

Bart backed against him. "Yep."

The Indians hadn't figured on the youngsters and the women. When they began to circle Jeb and Bart, Katie picked one off from the roof. Hoot came to the corner of the cabin and shot a horse out from under its rider. Jeb shot the Indian who was on foot. The daring attack didn't last long. The Indians were not well-armed. Only one or two carried guns. The rest used bows and arrows.

When the smoke cleared, four Indians lay dead. The other two gave up the fight and raced away into the woods.

Burris was one of the men killed.

Sparrow identified one of the others as her former lover and Hoot's father.

Jeb hoped it would be the end of the trouble. "I'll tote Burris to Fort Worth and collect my pay. Then head back to Indian Territory."

"Do you really think this woman, Fooswah, is my aunt?" Bart asked.

"I'd bet money on it."

"You say it's right pretty country, good grass, good water, and rolling hills?"

Jeb nodded. "Yes, it's mighty nice."

"Nancy," Bart said, "let's go with Jeb and meet my aunt. The cattle drives have probably started. We can travel along with one."

Nancy looked shocked. "Bart Jamison, are you crazy? What'll happen to our livestock and my chickens?"

"We'll come up with a plan," Bart replied. "I think it would be fun to go before we get old and set in our ways."

"I'll stay home and take care of things," Toby offered.

"I stay, too," Sparrow stated.

"Let me have a few days to think on this," Nancy grumbled and then turned toward Toby and Sparrow. "You two aren't much help."

"I go with Pa," Sam announced. "Ride Ace."

Jeb secured Burris' body across the back of an Indian pony and then threw a saddle on Brownie.

Bart walked up and handed him a roll of cash. "Buy enough supplies for my crew, too."

"You sure? Nancy don't seem too taken with the idea."

"She'll come around."

Jeb stood with his hand on the cinch. "I'd best take the wagon, if that's okay with you."

Bart nodded. "Probably be best, but we'll use pack horses for the trip. You keep a sharp eye out."

* * * * *

Part V

Russ

CHAPTER 23

RUSS still longed for Jeb's return, but thought of him less often now.

He spent most of his time in the garden, either pulling grass or keeping varmints from destroying the growing vegetables. In his spare time, he roamed the woods.

Sometimes local boys gathered to play a game of hide-and-seek that involved stalking and tracking. Russ was good at avoiding being found, although this appeared to perplex the other boys. If all else failed and they couldn't find him, they untied Tulip. From her tracking abilities, one would think she was part bloodhound. She would run around the edge of the woods and then take off in a certain direction. Although Russ asked her to be quiet, she brayed her loudest, announcing that her buddy was found. The little burro loved to play with the boys, especially if they happened to have a bit of bread to share.

Every morning at the breakfast table Russ and Fooswah practiced their language skills. He picked an object and said what it was called in English. Fooswah repeated after him and then said the name in Creek. Each day he learned more Creek and began to understand his playmates without using sign language. Fooswah seemed reluctant when speaking English, as if she was betraying those who saved her. Russ didn't doubt that she could say about whatever she wanted to in either language.

Birds sang, flowers bloomed, and animals frolicked as the weather warmed and spring pushed toward summer.

With Osekee's help, Russ built a rail fence around an area for Outlaw and Tulip, so they could graze freely. It wasn't much of a pen, but so far the animals didn't seem inclined to go elsewhere.

The pigs were always getting out, seeking new growth along the creek or in the garden. They had a big time rooting and eating everything they could find. The only way to protect the vegetables was to spend the night patrolling the garden. Russ suggested they butcher the pigs now instead of waiting until fall, but Fooswah disagreed. They took turns watching the garden, until Russ and Osekee could fix the hog-pen fence. A few nights sleep would be nice, but probably wouldn't last long. Those two pigs were master escape artists.

One warm afternoon Russ and his friends grew tired of hunting each other and decided to try their luck at fishing, the hard way. The trick was to find a shallow area where fish got trapped and couldn't return to deeper water. Once a fish was located, someone waded in and grabbed it by hand. This made Russ nervous, because he couldn't swim and didn't want the other boys to know.

Osekee found a deep hole beneath an undercut of the river bank. Some of the braver lads explored the pool, hoping to find a fish or two. Russ couldn't believe how long Osekee could stay under water. Several times he was sure his friend had drowned.

One of the boys came up and gave a shout. A big fish had been found. Now they had to figure out how to get it out of the water.

They were soon joined by an older boy named Bo, who began giving orders and pushing around the smaller guys. He was the one who had hit Tulip with a stick. Russ didn't like or trust him.

When Russ voiced his objections, the bigger and stronger Bo picked him up and threw him into the deep water. As he went under, Russ panicked. He thrashed about with his arms and struggled to get his head above water. Osekee jumped in to help. In his panic Russ pulled him down, too. Tulip brayed in the background, which scared him even more. He didn't want her to jump into the deep pool after him.

A big hand grabbed him by the arm and up he went. It was Owen Hunter. He and some of his children had been out hunting wild onions, when they heard the commotion and ran to help.

Russ coughed and sputtered.

"What were you doing in there, if you can't swim?" Owen asked.

"I'm not sure." Russ sensed that telling on Bo might make the bigger boy mad enough to retaliate. "I was watching from above, and next thing I knew I was going under. Thanks for saving me."

"You'd best learn to swim," Owen warned. "I'd give you a few lessons if I had time. The boys will help you. I have to get back to the post. Bo, did you find any onions?

Bo shook his head no.

"Then get to looking," Owen ordered. "You'd best bring home a good mess."

When Owen was well out of sight, Bo picked up an empty bucket and with slumping shoulders headed into the woods.

"Let's go help him," Russ said without a thought.

He drew puzzled looks from the other boys, but soon they all began hunting the delicate onions.

Unsure what to look for or where to look, Russ watched Osekee and Bo. With tops that looked like thin blades of grass, the tiny onions grew in damp areas. The boys scattered through the woods and shouted each time a large patch was found. In very little time, they almost filled the bucket.

Bo looked at Russ. "Mado." Taking a braided leather necklace from his neck, he put it on Russ and walked away, carrying the onion basket.

Osekee clapped Russ on the shoulder. "New friend."

Russ shrugged in doubt. "Race you to the cabin!"

It was a close contest between the boys, but Tulip was the one who brayed in victory.

Fooswah was in the garden pulling weeds, when they came rushing up. The boys collapsed, as if dead. She smiled at them and then laughed out loud when Tulip also dropped to the ground.

After catching his breath, Russ went to care for the pigs. He was a little puzzled that Osekee didn't accompany him. When he looked back, he saw Osekee and Fooswah in serious conversation.

The next morning Fooswah motioned for him. He joined her and away to the creek they went. It didn't take long for him to figure out what she and Osekee had discussed.

In a short time Fooswah taught him to float. She then demonstrated how to kick his legs and paddle with his arms. The elderly woman swam like a fish, and he tried hard to do as she did. After what seemed like hours, he could keep his head above water, but that was about all.

The next Sunday there was a big dinner at the church. Russ learned it was a celebration of spring and the reason for gathering the wild onions. Fooswah, who had also gathered onions, spent that morning cleaning a bunch. Then she cooked beans and made fry bread.

Russ carried the bucket of beans, while Fooswah toted the bread and onions. Once at the church she handed the onions to one of the other women. Curious to see what they did with them, Russ watched while they were added to a skillet of eggs. If he hadn't known what was in the bowl, he wouldn't have eaten any. The mixture was the color of cow manure. He didn't care for the egg and onions concoction, nor for the blue bread which resembled dumplings. Hominy, fry bread, and salt pork were his favorite dishes. It was a lovely day filled with good food and celebration.

The next morning, they went to the creek for swimming lessons. Russ was becoming comfortable in the water. It was a glorious day when he dove into the water and raced Fooswah across the creek and back. Of course, it was a narrow creek. No longer would fear keep him from joining his friends in their fishing adventures.

Spring was in full swing with birds chirping, trees budding, grass growing, and flowers waiting for the warmth of May to reveal their many colors. Russ grew almost as quickly as the grass. Fooswah gave up making britches for him, so like his friends he now wore a breech cloth. His skin became darker each day, but he would never pass for an Indian.

The garden continued to grow well, as did the weeds. Fooswah fussed every time she saw a weed and attacked it with a hoe or pulled it by hand. It became Russ' job to keep the dirt pulled up around the growing plants. It was a no-no for the roots to become visible. Watering was also necessary at times. Russ could now carry two buckets at a time.

They were busy one morning hoeing and pulling weeds, when a sudden stillness surrounded them.

"Storm," Fooswah said.

They gathered the tools and ran for the cabin. Thunder rumbled in the distance, and lightning danced across the sky. It was beautiful to watch, but scary to wonder what was headed their way.

To make sure Tulip and Outlaw were safe from lightning, Russ went back and secured them in the lean-to. He returned to the porch just as it began to pour down rain.

It stormed and rained for the next three days. Rain stopped on the fourth day, but storm clouds continued to build in the southwest.

The garden now stood in water. The pigpen was flooded, causing the pigs to huddle on a tiny bit of dirt. If it rained any more, they would have to be moved.

Russ decided to move the pigs to the lean-to with Tulip and Outlaw. They could stay in the empty stall, but he would have to re-enforce one side with some hog wire.

He got the fat pigs relocated and was brushing Tulip when Fooswah called for him. He joined her on the porch.

"Listen," she said.

There was a steady roar coming from the river. If it flooded, many homes would be lost, spring crops would be destroyed, and lives would be in jeopardy.

* * * * *

CHAPTER 24

WATER stood everywhere, and rain continued to fall.

So far, the cabin remained dry, but water lapped at the edge of the porch. It was almost up to Russ' knees when he went to feed the animals. Once that chore was done, he waded back to the cabin.

He kept a small fire going in the fireplace to knock the chill out of the room. Fooswah sewed and cooked, pausing occasionally to check the level of the water. Russ suspected she was afraid the roaring river was going to flood.

After four days it stopped raining, and the sun came out. The creek near the house had overflowed its banks, carrying all kinds of debris in its wake, much of which lay lodged against the pigpen fence. Everything was a wet, muddy mess.

When Russ let Tulip and Outlaw out of the lean-to, they sought higher ground where grass showed.

Together Fooswah and Russ sloshed to the garden. Only the corn was visible above the standing water.

"Maybe it will be okay when it dries up some," Russ suggested.

"Do over," was all Fooswah said.

The rain seemed to have stopped, but there was still a possibility the river would flood. Russ and Fooswah went to see how high it was. Along the path water ran in little rivulets or stood in puddles. The river rolled close edge of what had been a steep bank. Up-rooted trees swirled like mere twigs in the fast-moving water. Russ backed away from the frightful scene. It was hard to believe just a few days ago he and his buddies had played there.

It was a wet, wet world. Everything was either damp or soaked. Thank goodness for the sunshine. In a few days the muck would dry up, and then the clean-up could begin. Moisture was always welcomed, but preferred in smaller amounts spaced out over time. Too bad they couldn't bottle up the extra and save it for the hot, dry summer.

The first order of business was to hang out the bedding to rid it of the dampness. The door and lone window were opened to let in the warmth of the sunshine. Several buckets of water later the cabin floor was scrubbed clean. Once the cabin was in order and the bedding turned and re-hung, Russ went to muck out the lean-to.

Talk about a mess. One step and Russ found himself mired in the mud. Realizing it would take forever for the shaded shed to dry out, he tethered Outlaw and Tulip outside on a drier place near the cabin. The pigs would be moved after he got the fence cleaned and secured. It looked like there wouldn't be any hunting or fishing for a while. Discouraged, he walked back to the cabin to get slop for the pigs. They met him in their usual happy mood and promptly turned over their feed trough. Russ climbed into the stall and once again sank up to his knees in muck. When he finally got unstuck and the trough righted, Fooswah called him in for supper.

Before darkness fell, they gathered in the bedding. Sunshine had given the blankets a fresh smell. As Russ climbed into his clean, comfortable bed, he tried to ignore the disturbing sound of the roaring river.

The next morning the sun shined, and the roaring had ceased.

Fooswah beckoned to Russ. They made their way to the garden, both carrying a hoe. Russ watched the little woman make trenches to run the water away from the plants, and then took over the task. The corn was still standing, but had begun to turn yellow from too much moisture. If the sun continued to shine, there was a chance it would recover. The squash, beans, and potatoes looked ruined.

It was a sad pair who walked back to the cabin.

Days passed. Other than needing to replant the garden, things got back to normal. Russ spent two days cleaning the lean-to and getting the pigpen back in order. The pigs didn't care where they lived, as long as supper showed up every evening.

Russ forgot about playing with his friends and helped Fooswah in the garden. They managed to save most of the corn by turning the wet soil often, so that it would dry. The other vegetables didn't make it, so they would have to be replanted. He felt sorry for Fooswah. She seemed sad and worried, as she took the last of her seeds and carefully put them in the prepared ground. They would have to go to the post and hope to find seed potatoes. Maybe Owen had some.

Russ had not realized how much time had passed, until one day he noticed the world around him had changed. Grass grew green and tall. Colorful flowers bloomed. Birds sang. Inserts buzzed.

Although rain caused problems, it also brought beauty and a muddy burro. Tulip looked like a dirt dauber's nest.

"Come on, you filthy varmint. Let's give you a bath." Russ headed for the creek.

Tulip didn't really care for the cold water and scampered away. Russ brought her back and explained the necessity of being clean. He finally got her scrubbed, only to have her shake like a wet dog and roll in the grass. "Oh well, I can brush off the grass. Roll all you want."

The burro gave him a few dirty looks, and then she found a nice patch of green grass. She was grazing away, when Russ went to the cabin.

He called to Fooswah, but she didn't answer. Puzzled, he walked inside and spotted her lying on her bed.

"Fooswah, are you sick?" he asked.

She moaned and put her hand to her head.

Russ touched her forehead and jerked back his hand. "You're burning up! I'm going to get help."

Before he left, he wet a rag and laid it on her head.

"Mado," she whispered with a smile.

Outlaw hadn't been ridden in a while, so he was not cooperating. Russ struggled to catch him, and then he wouldn't take the bit. He must have battled with the horse for fifteen minutes before getting the saddle on him.

Worried and worn out, the youngster finally mounted. The frisky horse bowed up and began to pitch. Wonder of wonders, Russ managed to stay aboard. Outlaw didn't object to the fast trip to the trading post.

Russ hit the door at a run. "Mr. Hunter, Fooswah's sick!"

Owen Hunter came from the back. "What's the matter with her?"

"She's hot to touch and moaning."

"Let me get a few things, and we'll go check on her. Maybe I should take Hoktee, so she can stay and help you."

In a short time, Owen, Russ, and Hoktee rode to the cabin. Russ paced, while Owen examined Fooswah. He took some kind of medicine from a bag and spooned it into Fooswah's mouth, all the while explaining to Hoktee how to do it and how often. When he had done all he could, he motioned Russ outside.

"She has a bad fever," Owen explained. "Don't know what from, but it's serious. You'll have to watch her close. Feed her broth and plenty of water. Just to be safe, boil water for both of you to drink."

"How come?" Russ asked.

"Sometimes after a big rain the creeks get foreign matter in them that's not good for us. If you boil the water, it gets rid of the bad stuff."

"I'll boil some right now, so it'll be ready when she gets thirsty."

"That's the spirit. There's not much we can do but wait and hope. I'll be on my way. Hoktee will stay and help you."

"Thank you, Mr. Hunter."

"You're welcome. Let me know how she's doing."

"Okay."

When Owen left, Russ sat down on the porch step and cried hard, bitter tears. He couldn't imagine life without Fooswah. She was so kind and gentle.

"Please God, don't take her from me," he prayed. "If you take her, I won't have anybody."

Tulip came to Russ and stood nearby, as if to say *you still have me*. The sad boy went to the little burro and held her close. "We're not helping her by sitting here crying. Let's go see if the garden needs hoeing."

Days passed in a blur. Russ worked harder than ever to keep the garden alive. He knew how important it was to Fooswah. Many times a day he checked on her only to find her sleeping. Every night he sat with her and talked to her, explaining what he'd done that day. Hoktee often sat with them and offered comfort.

After five long days, Fooswah began to show some life. She tried to sit up in bed, but struggled. Russ ran to her side and helped. She offered a slim smile and patted his face. He was so happy that tears fell, and Fooswah took him into her arms. For a minute they held each other.

Hoktee smiled. "Broth?"

Fooswah nodded.

Although very weak, Fooswah improved daily and soon could sit on the porch in the warm sunshine.

Russ continued to boil their water and take care of the garden. It was a happy day when the frail woman walked to the garden with him. The smile on her face told him everything he needed to know.

"You saved us," she said. "We will have food."

Russ returned to his life of hunting, fishing, and playing with his friends. He also spent several days picking berries, which meant a constant battle against biting insects, snakes, and sharp thorns, but a fresh, berry cobbler made the job worthwhile. He learned to head to the creek with a bar of lye soap after a day in the berry patch. A good scrubbing would discourage the dreaded chiggers.

All was well in his world, but he often wondered about Jeb.

Is he coming back? Is he alive? Will he bring me a pony?

* * * * *

CHAPTER 25

SPRING passed into summer.

Despite pigs, varmints, floods, and insects, the garden flourished with fresh vegetables. Especially important was the bountiful corn crop, which was the staple food for the Creeks.

When the corn silks turned brown, the corn was ready to harvest.

Fooswah cautioned Russ to pull back the husks and check the kernels. They should be filled out before taking an ear of corn from the stalk. They were careful to pick only the ripe ears and leave the rest to mature.

Russ wanted to sink his teeth into those rich kernels filled with sweetness, but learned that no corn would be eaten until after the Green Corn Ceremony which was held each year in late June or early July.

In accordance with preparations for the ceremony, all old clothing, discarded items, and such were gathered and taken to a spot to be burned. Houses were cleaned and new clothing made. Russ didn't know what to make of all this, but gladly pitched in to help. He wasn't as eager to take the medicine Fooswah gave him to clean his intestines. She took some too, and both were sick at their stomachs for a few hours.

Tulip wasn't left out of the cleanse. Fooswah chopped up twist tobacco and put in her feed. The ornery burro spent half the day carefully pushing the tobacco to one side. Fooswah tried again by mixing a bit of sorghum with the feed. That trick worked. Tulip didn't seem to suffer any ill effects from the treatment, but afterwards she kept a close eye on Fooswah.

Russ was puzzled when Fooswah sent him to look for empty box turtle shells. He understood when the shells were made into rattles by partially filling them with small rocks. They would then be tied to dancer's legs. Fooswah demonstrated the steps to the dance. Russ caught on fast and the two danced, rattled, and laughed for several minutes.

The ceremony was held on the Creek ceremonial grounds and lasted several days. During this time the people dressed in their native costumes. Russ couldn't believe the beautiful colors, the painted faces, and elaborate headdresses. There were dancing, games, and feasting, as well as serious meetings concerning tribal matters. Russ enjoyed the ceremony and even danced a little. The Ribbon Dance, performed by the women and girls, was his favorite. It was an exciting time. The only musical instrument used was a drum, yet beautiful music was made by the dancers who wore bells and rattles and danced in perfect rhythm.

Fooswah explained how, in this time of celebration and starting anew, that all transgressions were forgiven except for murder. He wondered if some might be guilty of murder, when he watched a stickball game. It was a brutal sport, that ended up with the teams in a fight. No, a brawl. He climbed a tree and sat well out of range of a stickball racket.

* * *

RUSS enjoyed the celebrations, but was glad when they returned home.

The garden was still producing, but with the dry, hot weather wouldn't be for long. He toted water in the evening, hoping the cooler temperature at night would help the plants survive.

Every morning after their chores were done, Fooswah and Russ went to the woods to pick berries and plants to be eaten or used for medicine. Somedays he would skip the berry picking and fish, while Fooswah hunted her treasures. The secret to fishing in the hot summer was to find a deep, shaded pool of water and drop bait to the bottom. Sometimes Russ waited so long for a bite, that he would fall half-asleep. One tug on the pole meant the fish was just checking out things. A second tug signaled the fish was interested. After a third tug, Russ set the hook and often jerked a nice catfish out of the water.

The days became long and hot. Chores were done early in the morning, when there was a little cool air. Nothing much moved in the middle of the day. Fooswah and Russ usually sat in the shade of a hackberry tree and shelled corn or peas.

Twice a week she joined the other ladies near the post. They worked at various tasks, preparing for the winter. Everything grown was shared by the community. Many hours were spent grinding corn into a coarse meal or soaking it in lye water so the outer hull could be removed from the kernel and made into hominy. Now Russ understood why Fooswah saved ashes from the fireplace and wood stove. She mixed ashes and water to make lye.

Despite the heat, Russ and his friends gathered at the river to swim or fish. Tulip went with them, but usually was content to stand under a shade tree and doze. Bo came to love the burro, but she remained suspicious. He gained favor by bringing her bread, and finally she let him pet her.

* * *

ONE hot afternoon the boys decided to swim in the creek. Their favorite spot was a deep hole shaded by a large willow tree. Osekee jumped in first and hollered for his friends to join him.

Bo jumped in and grabbed a low hanging willow branch. A large cottonmouth water moccasin fell from the branch and landed on Bo's shoulder. As he reached to knock it off, the snake bit him on the hand.

Osekee, who was still in the water, grabbed Bo and pulled him toward the bank. The dark-brown, stubby reptile rushed after them, mad from having been disturbed. Russ and the other boys ran to the water's edge and began throwing rocks, sticks, and whatever they could find to turn away the mad critter. When the snake opened his mouth to strike at a stick, Russ understood the name cottonmouth.

Sitting Bo on the sand, Osekee examined his hand. Two fang marks on his right hand meant the snake was poisonous.

Russ called Tulip. When she trotted over, he explained that Bo needed a ride to the post. She seemed to understand, because Russ helped Bo onto her back and for once she didn't attempt to buck.

"Go tell Fooswah," Russ told Osekee. "I'll get Bo home, so someone can help him." Then he turned to the other boys. "Run tell Mr. Hunter what happened."

Owen Hunter met them halfway to the post. "Where is he bit?"

"On the hand," Russ answered.

Once at the post Bo was carried inside, so his mother and some of the other women could try to help him. The medicine man also came.

The boys sat outside on the porch steps, silent and somber.

Russ was relieved when Fooswah and Osekee arrived. She joined the boys, but was soon called inside the house.

The only doctor was at least three hours away. In a matter of minutes, Owen Hunter left the post, riding one horse and leading another. Russ hoped he could find the doctor in time.

People began drifting in to sit with the boys and wait for news. Soon a chant began. It was comforting in one way, but nerve-racking in another. Time passed. One of the women came from inside to tell them Bo was very sick, but still alive. With each passing hour hope grew stronger for Owen to get back with a doctor.

Daylight faded, and there was no change in Bo's condition. His arm was swollen twice its size and started to turn black. Russ learned that if the poison reached his heart, he would die.

Russ and Tulip headed home to feed Outlaw and the pigs. Once back at the cabin, he took care of his chores.

With reluctance he returned to the post, afraid of what he would find. He wasn't sure how many hours had passed. It felt like days. Maybe Owen had found the doctor, and they were with Bo.

However, the situation hadn't changed. As Russ rejoined his friends on the porch, the sun sank in the western sky. The hot day became a hot evening without a breath of air stirring.

Russ couldn't believe this was happening. They swam in that hole all the time. Snakes usually took off and didn't bother them. This was the first time one had fallen out of a tree. If he went swimming again, he'd make sure there were no snakes around.

Owen and another man rode in, but instead of a doctor Owen had found a trapper who knew how to treat snake bites. The man went inside with Bo.

Minutes later word came his treatment wasn't what everyone hoped.

To save the boy's life, he would have to cut off his hand.

* * * * *

CHAPTER 26

THE stillness of the night was broken by a mournful wail.

Russ covered his ears, when more cries joined the first.

The trapper came out onto the porch, sat on the top step, and shook his head. "There was another bite on his foot. No way I could save him."

Fooswah came from the house and motioned for Russ to join her. No words were spoken, as they made their way home. Tulip walked close beside Russ, and he often reached out to touch her. He was glad it was dark, so his tears weren't visible.

Early the next morning, Fooswah scurried around the kitchen cooking a variety of foods.

"Why are you cooking so much?" Russ asked.

"Feed people," was her response.

Russ helped by keeping the water bucket filled. He was making a trip from the creek, when Owen Hunter came riding up to the cabin. He sat down on the porch. Russ joined him.

Owen thanked Russ for helping Bo. "I figure you're going to be a bit confused by the burial customs, so I'd best explain them to you. Because the number four is so important to the people, someone will stay with Bo's body round the clock for four days."

"Why is four so important?" Russ asked.

"Four seasons, four directions. Earth, wind, sun, and water come to mind. There might be other things. The night before the burial, friends and family will sit all night with Bo and tell stories about him. They will place his personal items and food in the casket. This is called a wake. The day of the burial, gravediggers arise with the sun and dig the grave. They remain at the site to fill the hole. Friends and family members throw a handful of dirt onto the casket. This is known as the final handshake. A house will be placed over the grave as a symbol of family, home, and a place to which the spirit can return. Do you have any questions?"

"No, sir. Thank you for explaining what is going to happen. I didn't like Bo at first, but we became friends. I'll miss him."

Owen patted Russ on the shoulder. "Me, too."

Russ felt it his duty as Bo's friend to do his part, which right now was carrying water for cooking and for washing clothes. He must have made a million trips to the creek, and every trip he was terrified of getting snake bit. Russ vowed he would never go swimming again.

Time passed and with it the need to resume everyday life.

Osekee came carrying his fishing pole. Russ joined him, and they headed to the river. Using their long cane poles, they thrashed the grass and weeds to scare away snakes. They found a deep hole in a shaded area. Russ checked the tree limbs, while Osekee baited their hooks. Finally, both sat and tossed their lines into the water. Despite having checked all around, both boys kept watch on the area. It was not an enjoyable outing, especially since the fish weren't biting. With Tulip leading, they trudged home.

Hot summer days limited their activities. Most of the time was spent under a shade tree hoping for a cool breeze. In search of relief from the heat, the boys finally sought a new swimming hole. They searched for cool places near the creek, but never returned to their favorite spot.

One afternoon, Russ, Osekee, and Tulip traveled a good way down the creek to a new place they wanted to try. There was shade, but the tree limbs were high above the water. The only grassy area was some distance from the deep end of the pool. There was even a sandy place to sit on. Still cautious, the boys searched thoroughly before wading in. The only brave one was Tulip. She stood deep enough in the water to cool her belly. The boys joined her and decided she would make a good diving board. Russ climbed up onto her back and dove into the water. Osekee gave it try. Tulip tolerated them for a few dives and then walked out. She refused to return, even though they begged and tried to bribe her with bread, which she knew they didn't have.

The little burro grazed near the pool. Russ and Osekee dove for rocks or rested in the shade. Late in the afternoon, Tulip came to the edge of the pool and brayed.

"Come on in," Russ called. "We won't bother you."

Tulip brayed again and walked away into the woods. Russ watched her, but didn't get out of the water. She returned, brayed, and left again.

"Something's wrong," Russ said. "Let's go see what's bothering her."

Tulip picked up her pace, when she realized Russ was behind her. She went to a large cottonwood tree and stopped.

Russ rushed to her and looked around. "What is it, girl? I don't see anything."

They walked farther into the trees and found a lone wagon. There was no movement, no sound. The team was picketed nearby. The ground was bare, because the grass had been eaten to the nub.

Russ approached the wagon cautiously. "Hello?"

From inside there came a whimpering sound.

He lifted the back flap and looked inside. A man and woman lay dead in the wagon bed, and sitting between them was a baby. The little one went from whimpering to crying. When she saw Russ, she lifted her arms.

The bodies were beginning to smell, but Russ made himself go inside and get the baby. She was wet, dirty, and probably very hungry. He handed her to Osekee and climbed out of the wagon. They got away as quickly as possible.

"Let's get her to the cabin. Fooswah will know what to do. Poor little thing is probably starved."

Russ started carrying her, but soon gave her to Osekee. They took turns all the way back. Tulip ran ahead and brayed at the cabin door.

Fooswah came to the porch and spotted the boys headed her way.

"We found a baby," Russ said. "Her ma and pa are dead."

Fooswah took the little one from him, cradled her in her arms, and carried her into the cabin. She mixed some kind of mush, but didn't have much luck getting the baby to eat. Russ toted water and put some on to heat so they could bathe her.

"What are we going to do with her?" Russ asked.

"Tell Owen," Fooswah replied. "Need milk."

Russ saddled Outlaw, while Osekee waited on the mounting stump. Once they were both mounted, Tulip led the way. A few crackers always awaited her at the post.

Although Russ wanted to hurry, he knew better than to run Outlaw in the heat of the day. He did kick him into a trot, but not for long.

Once at the trading post, Russ slipped off Outlaw and dashed inside. "Mr. Hunter! We need some milk for the baby!"

"What in the world ails you, boy?" Owen asked. "What baby?"

"Me and Osekee found a baby in a wagon. Her folks are dead."

"I'd best go back with you to find out what's going on. Let me see if I can find a wet nurse for the baby."

"She don't need a nurse. She needs milk."

Owen laughed. "Okay. I'll check about some milk. You fellas go on back and tell Fooswah I'm coming."

* * *

ONCE home, Russ and Osekee put Outlaw in the pasture and then hurried to the cabin.

They ran onto the porch like a herd of stampeding buffalo. Fooswah met them with a stern look and a finger to her lips.

Owen rode in a little while later, accompanied by a young woman holding an infant. Everyone went inside and gathered round the baby who lay on Fooswah's bed.

"Well, ain't she pretty. Wonder what in the world happened?" Owen scratched his head. "Lily's going to nurse her for you, until we can find a milk cow. I think Homer has a fresh cow I can get, but it may take a day or two."

The baby woke up and started to cry. Lily picked her up and put her to a breast. The crying stopped.

"Well, folks, looks like you have another mouth to feed. I'll help you all I can, until we can find a home for her. Russ, while I try to find a milk cow, you'll have to tote her to Lily a few times a day so she can nurse. Can you do that?"

"Yes, sir."

* * *

OWEN rode out to the wagon.

He searched through the couple's belongings to try to learn who they were. A letter in the man's pocket was addressed to John Anderson. Owen took the letter in hopes of notifying their kin.

Although he hated to do it, out of caution everything was burned.

Leading the team, he rode away from the scene.

He hoped the couple had died of food poisoning or bad water. If it was a disease of some kind, the baby might get sick and infect others.

He shivered at the thought.

* * * * *

CHAPTER 27

RUSS was amazed at how much work a baby required.

He toted water to and from the creek. Several times a day he took the baby, now called Summer, to the village.

At first he mounted Outlaw and had Fooswah hand Summer up to him. By the time he got to Lily's, both he and Summer were screaming.

Owen saved the day by hitching Tulip to a little cart. Fooswah placed a blanket in the bottom and lay the baby on it. Russ walked beside Tulip. The big problem was the heat, so they tried to go early in the morning and late in the evening. Fooswah fed Summer mush in between trips.

Along with the necessary trips was diaper detail. Fooswah made several but needed many more. Russ seemed to always be hanging them out on the line or soaking them in hot water. He looked forward to the day Mr. Hunter would bring the milk cow.

Several days went by before Russ saw Owen Hunter riding down the lane with a milk cow trailing behind him on a lead rope. A small calf followed its mother.

"Hi, Mr. Hunter. Thanks for bringing the cow."

"You may not be thanking me after you try milking."

As it turned out, Mr. Hunter was right. The cow was docile enough, but Russ couldn't get the knack. The cow got irritated after standing for a long spell and started moving around. She stepped on Russ' foot and stood there still as could be. He pushed and hollered at her, but she remained planted, chewing her cud. Finally, Mr. Hunter moved her enough for Russ to get free.

"Put a little feed in the trough," the older man suggested. "Maybe that will help."

The cow appreciated the grain, but it didn't last near long enough. Mr. Hunter finally took over and got about a quart of milk in the bucket.

Who would have thought milking would be such hard work?

"Remember to place your thumb and forefinger on a tit up close to the cow's bag," Owen instructed. "Then gently pull down and squeeze with all your fingers. You'll catch on after a while."

"I just hope Summer don't starve to death waiting on me."

The calf was a big problem. It had to be separated from the cow at night, so she'd have plenty of milk. The next morning the calf would be allowed to nurse for a few minutes to get the milk flowing. Once the little guy got started, it was hard to get him out of the stall into another pen. Russ usually got stepped on and sometimes knocked down. After putting up the calf, he set out a little grain for the cow. He sat on the one-legged stool, placed his head against her flank, and began the worrisome chore.

The first few days were torture, but he managed to get enough milk for Summer. Mr. Hunter had brought a bottle. It was a strange-looking object, but it worked.

Twice a day Russ milked. One morning he yelled in triumph, scared the cow, and was knocked off his stool. With pride he carried a good three quarts of milk to the house. There was no way to keep it from spoiling, so the extra went to the pigs. They didn't complain.

Summer became the center of attention. Russ checked on her before he began his chores. Many mornings she would be awake playing with her feet or looking around. She rarely cried, and if she did someone picked her up. Although she was a lot of work, both Russ and Fooswah loved her. It was a glorious day when she crawled to a chair and stood. She would be walking soon.

Osekee came by once in a while, but Russ didn't have time for hunting or swimming. He sometimes longed to run with his friend to the swimming hole, but wouldn't leave. The fever Fooswah had suffered earlier in the summer had taken its toll on her. Although she now tired easily, she never complained.

On the days it got so hot that the cabin wasn't bearable, they walked to the creek and sought a shady spot. Russ sat in the shallow water with Summer. She loved to splash, kick, and squeal. Fooswah sat against a tree trunk and took a nap. Tulip always went with them, but stood in the shade as if hoping for a breeze.

Days passed, bringing more intense heat. The now dry and crisp grass was not much good for the animals. Russ often took Tulip and scouted for a shaded area, where some green grass remained. When they found such a place, he returned and brought the cow and Outlaw. The best spot he found was in a pecan tree grove near the river. The large trees provided much shade and grass. Fooswah and Summer went with him. Russ carried Summer piggy-back, which worked out well until she discovered his hair was fun to pull.

While the animals grazed, Fooswah placed Summer on a quilt to play, and Russ tried his luck at fishing. Most of the deep holes were dry, but getting to the main current was dangerous due to quicksand. He wandered around looking for a likely spot and then joined Summer on the quilt.

Russ often wondered how long Jeb had been gone. He was happy here and well cared for, but felt his place was with his ranger friend. What fun it would be to ride through open country and track outlaws. Maybe Jeb would let him carry a pistol. Sometimes he daydreamed of running down a bad guy and getting into a gun fight. He always got his man without having to shoot him. He didn't allow himself to think Jeb wasn't coming back. His buddy would return—someday.

* * *

ONE hot summer morning, Fooswah met Russ as he came from the lean-to with a bucket of milk.

"Look," she said pointing toward the south.

The sky in that direction was full of smoke. Russ handed Fooswah the bucket of milk and caught Outlaw.

"I'll go see what's happening," Russ said. "Be back in a little bit."

He found a large fire raging toward the trading post. If not stopped, it would come onto Fooswah's place. Men and women fought the blaze with wet sacks, blankets, shovels, or whatever they could find. In places where the dry grass was short, the fire could be put out, but the taller grass was a different story.

Russ spotted Owen Hunter and rode to him. "How can I help?"

"Ride to the church and ring the bell. When someone shows up, have them stay to warn folks about the fire. Alert as many as you can. Then ride back home. We're going to try backfiring. If that don't work, we're in trouble."

Russ raced away and did what Owen said to do. As soon as some folks came to the church and found out about the fire, they began backfiring around the brush arbor and the wooden building where worship service was held in the winter.

The minister asked Russ to ride and warn a little lady who lived nearby but was deaf.

"What's that mean?" Russ asked.

"She can't hear."

Without any hesitation, Russ headed in the direction he was told. The lady finally understood when he took her outside, and she saw the smoke. Once she was on her way, he rushed ahead of her.

Riding back into the church yard, Russ approached a man. "Is there anyone else I should check on?"

"No. You'd best go home and prepare to flee."

"Flee to where?"

"Go to the river. If the fire gets close, cross to the other side. The fire will stop at the river."

When Russ raced into the yard, Fooswah met him and handed him Summer. "Go to the river. I will follow with Tulip and the pigs."

"What about the milk cow?"

"Turn loose. Maybe she follow. Go."

Russ had no choice, but to do as she said. He rode away, worried sick about Fooswah.

Tulip didn't wait on the pigs. She stayed right behind Outlaw.

He was a relieved boy when two fat pigs and a frail little woman joined him and Summer.

If the fire came closer, they would cross a shallow channel to a sandbar in the middle of the river.

Huddled together, they waited and hoped the men could beat the beast that could destroy all they owned.

* * * * *

CHAPTER 28

FOOSWAH and Russ made a small camp near the edge of the river across from the sandbar.

Russ tethered Outlaw and then helped Fooswah spread a quilt on the sand in the shade of the tall river bank.

As soon as he sat down Summer, she headed for the water. Tulip grabbed her by the diaper and pulled her back onto the quilt. Summer squealed her displeasure and tried a new direction. The burro retrieved her again. This action continued, until Russ came to the rescue and sat the little one on Tulip's back. She patted her furry friend and laughed.

There was no milk for Summer, so Fooswah chewed jerky and put it into her mouth. Russ was appalled at first, but realized his mother probably had done the same for him. Although the baby was eating, she still needed milk. Maybe the milk cow would be okay. Animals had a way of taking care of themselves. He'd check as soon as it was safe.

As they sat for hours on their small quilt island, a million *what ifs* filled Russ' mind. What if the river started to rise? What if snakes came from the burning grass and sought refuge on the sandbar with them? What if the fire couldn't be stopped and Fooswah's cabin burned? What if the cow didn't escape and Summer didn't have milk? He needed to do something before he went crazy with worry.

"Hello!" Osekee hollered from the bank above them.

Russ jumped up and headed toward the embankment. "We're here!"

Osekee joined him and they returned to Fooswah. "The fire is burning itself out. We managed to save all of the dwellings, except the ones far out where there wasn't time to warn folks. We will help them rebuild."

"Can we go home now?" Russ asked.

"Yes. I'll help you." Osekee picked up Summer. The baby giggled and wiggled with delight and patted Osekee's face.

Russ helped Fooswah gather their supplies and then started up the steep embankment. Looking back, he realized she was too worn out to make the climb on her own. "I'll be right back to help you."

He carried the quilt up to the top and spread it on the ground. "Osekee, put Summer on the quilt. Then help me get Fooswah up here." He turned to the burro. "Tulip, watch the baby. We'll be right back."

With Osekee pushing and Russ pulling, they managed to get Fooswah to the top. Winded, they all sat down to recuperate.

Russ laughed when he saw Summer's diaper was almost off, because Tulip had pulled her back onto the quilt each time she had tried to escape. Tulip came to Russ as if to say she did her job. Russ promised her a piece of bread when they got to the cabin.

In the distance, they could see where the fire had been. Tree trunks still smoldered. It had come close to the lean-to and pigpen. Thankfully, the back-firing had worked.

Russ grabbed the slop bucket and mixed food for the pigs. They ran squealing behind him to their pen. Outlaw and Tulip were cared for next. The milk cow was nowhere to be seen. The grass was burned except right around the cabin. Maybe she tried to go back to her home.

Discouraged, Russ went to the cabin. Summer was howling for her bottle. Osekee tried to pacify her. He ran around the cabin with her and bounced her up and down on his knee. She continued to wail, until Fooswah fed her mush laced with honey.

"I can't find the cow and calf," Russ said.

"Try river. Look for tracks," Fooswah suggested.

Russ was disgusted with himself. Why hadn't he thought of looking for tracks?

"Come on, Osekee," he said hitting the door. "Help me look for the milk cow."

Once they started looking, her tracks weren't hard to find. She was smart enough to stay ahead of the fire and go to the river. When they found her, she was standing in the shade of a cottonwood chewing her cud. They started her toward home, only to have her turn back and head for the brush. Russ flushed her out, and Osekee pointed her in the right direction, but she rushed past him back toward the river. Both boys were worn out by the time they got her to the lean-to. The calf trailed along happy to be with its mama.

Russ tried milking her but came up with very little. The calf had sucked her dry. Summer wasn't going to be happy, although she was eating mush and food Fooswah chewed for her.

Summer was a pretty baby with light blond hair, sky-blue eyes, and a bubbly personality. Russ loved to hear her giggle or laugh, which she did often. He always checked on her first thing when he got up in the morning. Sometimes she was awake looking at him with those big, blue eyes and smiling from ear to ear. "I'll be back with some milk," he would explain, as he headed toward the lean-to. She always protested his leaving, so most times he picked her up and sat her on the floor. He knew she was wet and didn't even think about attempting to change her. Fooswah took care of that job. He couldn't imagine life without Summer.

Russ was surprised when Fooswah left the cabin after breakfast one morning in late summer. Curious, he trailed along. She went to the garden spot and began turning the ground with a spade.

"What are you doing?" Russ asked.

"Plant pea," Fooswah answered, as she continued turning the soil.

Russ had planned to go fishing with Osekee, but fell into working beside Fooswah. Summer played in the dirt near them. Tulip grazed close to the baby and would alert them if she crawled away. Osekee came soon after they began working, but instead of helping he played with Summer. It didn't take long to plant peas and turnips.

"Catch fish," Fooswah said to Russ.

"You want me to fish instead of helping you?"

Fooswah nodded and rubbed her belly. "Catch many fish."

That's all it took for Russ to join his friend. They were on their way to the river in a few minutes. Osekee located a pool of water, and they threw in their lines. Russ had just sat down, when he got a bite. He pulled out a nice catfish, and soon Osekee did, too. They made two trips to get their catch to the cabin.

While the boys cleaned the fish, Fooswah relit the fire in a smoldering pecan tree stump. The grass was charred all around it, but the stump would continue to burn for days. When Fooswah brought out wooden racks, Russ understood the reason for the fire. The fish was cut into strips that were hung on the racks in such a way the smoke would cover them.

Leaving the burned area, Russ gathered green limbs to create smoke.

"Catch more fish," Fooswah said.

Russ scratched his head, confused.

"Smoked fish will keep for a time," Osekee explained. "She's preparing for the winter. Tomorrow my mama will come help. Maybe Fooswah will share with us."

The boys fished, cleaned fish, and helped smoke fish, until Osekee's mother and siblings came to help. Then they returned to the river to catch more. Everyone worked hard. The more smoke the better, and green wood smoked best. Russ wasn't sure he would ever eat fish again. He was almost glad when they stopped biting.

* * *

LONG hot days grew shorter with cooler temperatures in the evenings and mornings. They were hoeing the garden one morning, when a big buck walked to the edge of the timber.

"Shoot deer," Fooswah said.

"How can I shoot a deer?" Russ asked. "My bow isn't strong enough, and the shotgun will tear it up."

"Tell Owen."

Later that day Russ saddled up and rode to the post.

After Russ explained what he needed, Owen brought out a rifle. "This Sharps should do the trick. It's old and heavy, but shoots straight. Come on. I'll teach you to use it."

They went out to a deep ditch and set up some empty cans. Owen explained how to load the gun and aim at the target. Russ expected it to kick like the shotgun, and it did. Shooting came naturally to him, and Owen ended his lesson. The main problem was holding up the gun long enough to aim it.

"I can't hold it steady," Russ complained.

"Find a low tree branch you can rest it on or a mound of dirt. Some hunters poke a forked stick in the ground and place the gun barrel in the fork. It's one thing to hit a can. Quite different to hit a deer. Remember to aim behind the front leg." He walked to Tulip and pointed to the place where Russ should try. "If you shoot the animal, don't rush up to it. Let it lay for a while. I've seen many a shot deer get up and run off if the shooter gets in a big hurry. If you wound one and it runs, there will be a blood trail to follow. Then there's the problem of getting it out of the woods. Maybe you can use your horse to tote it home. When you shoot a gun, you clean it. Come to the porch. I'll show you how. When you bag your deer, I'd appreciate enough venison for supper."

"What's venison?"

"Deer meat."

"I sure will, Mr. Hunter. Thank you kindly."

* * * * *

CHAPTER 29

THOUGHTS of deer ran through Russ' mind, as he rode away from the trading post.

He was only a short distance away when it occurred to him that he had no idea how to find a deer. Of course, he often saw one or two when he was out in the woods, but didn't know how to hunt them. Confused, he returned to the post. Owen Hunter was on the porch talking to a couple of men when Russ approached.

"How do you find a deer?" Russ asked, after the visitors had left.

"Go out in the woods and look for tracks. They usually have a path they travel to and from water. The river bottom is a good place for them to stay hidden, but it's hard to get one out of if you shoot it there. Best to find an open area surrounded by trees near the path they travel. Go out early in the morning or late in the evening and sit at the base of a tree. You must be very still. Become part of the tree. Patience is the key to success, so don't expect to get one on the first try."

"Thanks, Mr. Hunter. I'll go find a spot and see what happens." Russ once again turned to go home.

"Russ," Owen called after him, "don't load the gun until you're ready to shoot. Remember the bullet travels a long way, if you miss your target. It's plenty capable of killing a person or an animal far off. Aim careful and take your time."

"Okay."

Russ pondered how he could sit, hold up the gun, and aim. He needed something to prop the barrel on to keep it steady. Deer hunting might not be as easy as it sounded.

By the time he reached the cabin, his arms ached from carrying the heavy rifle. Wringing wet with sweat, his head hurt from the glare of the sun. He fell more than sat on the edge of the porch.

Tulip laid her head in his lap.

Russ rubbed her gently. "We're going deer hunting, but you have to be very still and quiet. Can you do that?"

Tulip sighed in answer.

Russ scouted for several days before he found a game trail that crossed an open area where the grass wasn't charred by fire. A large hackberry tree stood at one edge, a perfect place to shoot from. If he missed, the bullet wouldn't be apt to strike anything but a tree across the river.

Moving to and from his hunting area, he looked for a forked stick to serve as a prop for his rifle barrel. He found one, but couldn't get it stuck into the hard ground. For two days he soaked the ground with water he carried from the creek. Using a good-sized rock, he managed to drive the stick into the dirt. Satisfied with his work and hiding place, he decided to try his luck the next morning.

The birds hadn't come off their roosts when Russ left the cabin. He turned the calf in with its mother, but would take it out when he returned. He didn't figure to be gone long. The cow's bag would be full by evening. Summer was eating some now, but still wanted milk. He had mixed the pigs' food last night, so it would be ready this morning. Outlaw was no problem, and Tulip would come with him.

The sky grew lighter, while he made his way to the tree. Stars blinked out, as the sun peeked over the horizon. Russ made himself comfortable against the tree trunk and watched for deer. Tulip grazed nearby.

Time passed. A coyote loped across the meadow. A hawk circled far overhead. Squirrels chattered and fussed above him. It was so peaceful that Russ felt himself getting sleepy. He sat up straighter and told himself to pay attention.

The coyote came back into view. He started across the open area and then stopped, jumped straight up, and began digging in the dirt. Something went running away, and the coyote chased after it. A mouse or rat ran in circles, darted and dodged as the coyote tried to catch it. It was so funny to watch that Russ almost laughed out loud. In the end the rodent got away, leaving its tormentor still hungry.

Russ thought of a dozen things he needed to be doing at home. He finally convinced himself to give up and come back later. When he got up and started away from the tree, three deer ran off into the woods. He couldn't believe it. How had he not seen them? Tulip joined him, and Russ told her about his failure as a hunter.

Summer squealed in delight, when Russ walked into the cabin. He held her, while Fooswah fixed him something to eat. The baby was growing fast and learning new things every day. Her favorite buddy was Tulip. She loved to sit on her back, pulls her long ears, or tug on her tail.

For three days, Russ went to his tree and waited for a deer to cross his sights. All he had gotten so far was insect bites, a rash of poison ivy, and a dim view of hunting. Fooswah doctored the horrible, itchy rash and dabbed something on the bites, but there was nothing she could do about his hunting skills.

The weather began to change, bringing cooler mornings and evenings. Tree leaves faded from green into different colors, and squirrels gathered nuts. Animals were more active in the cool mornings. Russ saw turkeys, quail, coyotes, an occasional skunk but no deer until the morning of his sixth day out. He was watching a covey of quail come off their roost and begin feeding, when he caught movement from the corner of his eye.

Slowly, he turned his head. There stood a beautiful deer not more than thirty yards from him. Trying to contain his excitement, he aimed at the animal and pulled back the hammer on the rifle. His mouth felt like it was full of cotton, his hands were sweating, and he was sure the deer could hear his heart beating.

Taking a deep breath, he squeezed the trigger. *Click!* He had forgotten to load the gun. The perfect opportunity and he had botched it. Cussing under his breath, he watched the deer's white tail fade in the distance.

Not discouraged, Russ hunted morning and evening.

One day a deer appeared and stood still a little too long. Russ dropped it with one shot. He wanted to rush to the animal, but remembered to wait for several minutes. Tulip, however, didn't remember. She walked out to the downed deer and gave it a sniff. It must have been dead, because it didn't move. Russ checked to make sure he'd reloaded his gun, and then approached the animal with caution. Beautiful, sightless, brown eyes brought tears that blurred his vision. He felt horrible for having killed this harmless creature. Now perhaps Fooswah would be happy, and he could do some fun things with his friends. Plus it would be a tasty change from their usual meal of salt meat.

With Tulip beside him, Russ hurried to the cabin to tell Fooswah about his kill and to get Outlaw. Owen had suggested they haul the deer home on the horse, but Outlaw had a different opinion. When he smelled blood, he balked. No amount of effort changed his mind.

"Get Owen," Fooswah said.

* * *

"GREAT job!" Owen exclaimed when he saw the deer. "You picked out a nice fat doe and hit her in the right spot. I'll gut her here. The varmints will clean up everything in no time."

Once that chore was accomplished, Owen pointed to Outlaw. "Bring the horse over here and help me get her on him."

"He won't move," Russ explained.

Owen went to Outlaw. "Come on fella. We need your help."

With a firm hand he led the horse around the deer a few times, each time getting closer. Making sure the wind was blowing away from them so the scent wasn't as strong, they managed to load the dead doe. Outlaw acted so crazy Russ couldn't control him.

Owen got on his horse and rode to Russ. "Hand me the lead rope."

Russ handed him the rope, and he quickly wrapped it around his saddle horn. Snubbed to Owen's horse, Outlaw had to follow or have his neck stretched.

They hung the doe by her back legs from a tree limb. Owen cut her throat to let the blood drain, and he with Fooswah's help began skinning it. Russ watched Summer while they worked and was glad to be left out of the bloody job. Once that task was finished, they cut the carcass into portions. Most of the meat was cut into strips to be dried into jerky. The other parts could be fried or roasted.

Russ thought they were finished, until Fooswah cracked open the skull and collected the brains.

"Are we going to eat those?" he asked.

"No, use to tan hide," Fooswah explained.

He was shocked when she began collecting ligaments and tendons.

"Bow strings," she explained.

"Oh," was all he could think to say.

Owen tied a good portion of venison behind his saddle and then mounted his horse. "Holler when you get another one. I'll come help you dress it."

Russ was puzzled by the phrase 'dress it'. It looked to him like they had undressed it.

With a shrug, he headed to clean up, milk the cow, feed the animals, and then help Fooswah smoke the meat.

Walking to the lean-to, he thought of Jeb and how proud he would be of him. "I hope Jeb gets back before winter," Russ told Tulip.

She rubbed against his leg in agreement.

* * * * *

Part VI

Indian Territory

CHAPTER 30

THE trip to Fort Worth was uneventful.

Jeb met two farmers on his way, but no troublemakers. He knew all kinds of folks traveled to and from the town, and some of them weren't law-abiding.

His first stop was the office of Sheriff Jones. Because it was well into the night, the sheriff suggested they leave Burris in the wagon until daylight. Jeb had no choice but to agree to bring the already smelly body early the next morning.

The hostler at the livery stable was as reluctant as Jones about keeping Burris for the night. After some discussion, the wagon was left in the corral out back of the barn. Jeb slept in the hayloft. By morning, he was ready to dump the body and forget the reward. He fussed while he fed and groomed the horses.

"How about me leaving him here and letting the sheriff come get him?" Jeb asked the hostler.

"No way. You're lucky I let you spend the night. No telling how long it will take the law to get here, and that fella's getting ripe."

Jeb hitched up the team and drove to the sheriff's office. He noticed folks giving him plenty of space.

The sheriff came from the boarding house with a napkin still tucked in his collar. "Damn, man! Why didn't you leave him in the wagon yard?"

"Hostler wouldn't let me."

"Well, let's take a look and get this done with."

Jeb uncovered the body. "You ever seen him?"

"Got a glimpse of him once. He was a mean-looking son-of-a-gun."

"He lived up to his looks," Jeb said.

After a quick look, the sheriff backed up a couple of steps. "Well, you got him. I'll get the paperwork done and your money for you. Stop by later today. Drop the body at the cemetery. I'll get someone to take care of it."

"Okay, thanks. I'll see you later."

After getting rid of Burris, Jeb drove the wagon to the general store. He walked inside and started gathering provisions.

A pair of rough-looking characters watched him.

Paying no attention to them, he picked a handbill off the counter. It was an announcement for a musical event to be held in the hotel lobby that evening. What got his attention was the name of the featured violinist: George Washington Scott.

"Well, I'll be durned," Jeb said to the manager. "I know this guy."

"You'd better buy a ticket. I hear he's mighty good."

"Where do I get one?"

"Right here."

"Guess I'd best get a new outfit. Then a bath, shave, and haircut."

"I can handle the outfit. The barber's across the street. A little farther down there's a bathhouse."

"Okay, fix me up with some fancy duds. I'll pay you this afternoon, when I collect my money from the sheriff."

"You a bounty hunter?" one of the shady-looking men asked.

"No," Jeb replied. "I'm a Texas Ranger, if it's any of your business."

The man grunted and walked away.

"Watch those two," the store clerk cautioned. "They're usually up to no good."

"I seem to run into that kind a lot. Thanks for the warning."

With the clerk's help, Jeb picked out an outfit. He studied a bit and made a list of provisions for the clerk to fill.

"I hope I didn't forget anything. I'll be back later to pay you, but will pick up the supplies in the morning—if that's agreeable with you."

"That's fine. Enjoy the show."

Jeb drove the team back to the livery, unharnessed the horses, and led them to a stall. He paid for feed, hay, and an overnight stay.

With free time on his hands, he decided to visit the nearby horse and mule barn. The huge building housed hundreds of horses on one side and as many mules on the other.

He strolled over to watch the horse auction. A small pinto pony caught his eye. Before he knew it, he was raising his hand to up the bid. In a short time he bought the pony and wondered what possessed him. Thinking about Sam, he bid on another pony and won it. After a little dickering, he also picked up two kid's saddles. He walked away picturing the looks on two little guys' faces.

He led the ponies to the livery and paid for their stalls and feed. After collecting his money from the sheriff, he returned to the store to pick up his new outfit. It was time to get cleaned up and find a decent meal.

Walking around, he found Fort Worth to be a busy place and not a fort at all. From the stories he had heard, it started out as a military post but the soldiers were there only a few years. The deserted buildings were then used for various businesses. The town survived and prospered when cattle drives came right down main street. Once through town, the drive stopped for a few days near the Trinity River.

With the cattle came a bunch of rowdy, rough cowboys who were given part of their pay and time off to relax. The town became divided into two sections. The cowboys and buffalo hunters visited saloons, gambling houses, and bordellos in one area, while law-abiding folks occupied the other side. Law and order applied only to one side of town. There was no way to control a bunch of cowboys and buffalo hunters.

Jeb stayed on the peaceful side. The bathhouse was large with several rows of tubs surrounded by curtains, stacks of clean towels, and men to tote water. After soaking in a long, hot bath, he dressed in his new clothes and found the barber shop, which was another treat. Next he enjoyed a good meal at a nice boarding house cafe.

Feeling like a new man, Jeb thought about George Washington and that darn fiddle. It was too early for the performance, but maybe he could see George before the show.

As soon as he walked into the hotel, he spotted George sitting with a group of folks eating dinner. Not wanting to disturb him, Jeb sat down in the lounge area. He picked up a newspaper to try to catch up on the latest happenings.

"Jeb! Jeb Powers! Is that you?"

Jeb stood and was met with an exuberant bear hug. "Howdy G.W. How are you?"

"Thanks to you, I'm alive and well. What are you doing in these parts?"

"I finally caught Burris. Now I'm going back to get Russ."

The place began to fill with people, more folks than Jeb liked but they were mannerly and well-dressed.

"Follow me," George said.

Before he could balk, Jeb was sitting in the middle of the front row. When the performance started, he expected the kind of music played at country dances and barn raisings, but the program in his hand listed pieces by Mendelssohn, Bach, and Brahms—folks Jeb hadn't heard of. When George began to play, he sat mesmerized. It didn't matter who these guys were. Their music was wonderful, and Jeb enjoyed every note. He knew he would replay it all in his head many times.

The tough ranger was shocked and probably turned red around the ears, when George announced that the last song was dedicated to him. The audience stood to the lively tune of *The Yellow Rose of Texas*.

George met Jeb after the show. "Meet me for breakfast about daylight. I have to catch the early morning stage for Austin."

"How was Lillian when you left?" Jeb asked.

"Not good. Captain Webster was killed by Comanches."

The news shocked Jeb. "What's she going to do?"

"She didn't say," George replied.

* * * * *

CHAPTER 31

LONG after the stage left Fort Worth carrying George Washington, his last words remained in Jeb's mind. *She didn't say.*

Right then he decided to ride through Fort Sill on his way to Fooswah and Russ. If Lillian was still there, maybe he could help her.

Jeb went to the livery to check on the horses and ponies. They were fat and sassy and ready to travel. He hitched up the team and tied the little ones to the tailgate. It shouldn't take long to load the items he'd ordered.

Well before noon he left Fort Worth headed in the wrong direction. He'd noticed two men hanging around the store, as he loaded up supplies. It was same two he had seen yesterday when he went in to leave his list.

His new plan was to head for the Trinity River and fall in with a cattle drive. It would take him far from his original route, but maybe those varmints would lose his tracks.

For several miles he followed the chopped-up dirt left by the hooves of hundreds of cattle and horses, and then turned toward Bart's place. His rifle lay on the wagon seat beside him. He had one pistol snug in its holster with another one tucked under his vest.

Heat waves danced across dry grass, and dust surrounded the wagon. Just ahead was the creek where a few weeks ago Jeb had met a couple of arrows. He planned to water the team and ponies, and then rest for a bit.

The banks of the creek were cut away by the travel of wagons and animals, so it was a down-hill slope to the creek bed and an up-hill climb to the other side. Jeb started down the slope and met one of the outlaws at the bottom. The man sat on his horse holding a pistol, but the silly grin on his face irritated Jeb more than the gun.

"Drop your gun belt and step down mighty careful," the man said. "I'll take over for you."

"Sure thing," Jeb answered, as he unbuckled his gun belt.

When he turned to step down, he fell to the ground and rolled under the wagon into the shallow water. The surprised outlaw rode to one side firing a shot. Jeb shot him out of the saddle.

A bullet ricocheted off the wagon wheel.

Jeb crawled through the water and mud to the back of the wagon. The ponies pulled back on their ropes, trying to get loose. He talked to them, and they calmed some.

To draw the shooter's attention away from the wagon, Jeb ran down the creek bed, up the other side, and into a wooded area. The confused outlaw rushed into the open, trying to spot him. Jeb shot him in the arm. The man threw down his gun and ran. The sound of a fast-moving horse told Jeb he was safe.

He tied the dead man across his saddle and slapped the horse with his hat. He figured the trouble was over, but decided to travel a bit further before stopping. There was another creek crossing in a few miles.

It was late when Jeb finally reached Bart's place. Toby, Hoot, Katie, and Sam met him before he reached the barn and corral.

"Oh my gosh!" Katie ran her hands over the small horses. "What pretty ponies."

Toby stood, looking them over. "What you going to do with them? They're too little for most folks to ride."

"They're about thirteen hands. Just right for kids. I'm giving one to Sam and the other one to a little boy back in the territory."

Sam looked shocked. "My own horse?"

"Which one do you choose?" Nancy asked.

Sam pointed to the sorrel. "This one. Like Ace."

"What do you tell Jeb?"

"Thank you."

"You're welcome," Jeb replied with satisfaction.

The three older kids perked up, when Jeb handed each a pair of new boots.

"You're spoiling them," Bart said.

"I've got a surprise for you, too, big man, and for the beautiful ladies."

Nancy and Sparrow were thrilled with two bolts of material and yards of colorful ribbon. Bart proudly tried on his new, black hat and thanked Jeb as did the ladies. Last was a sack of sweets everyone enjoyed.

The next few days were spent preparing for a trip north. Bart decided on the horses to be used for riding and for pack animals. He and Jeb took them to Daniel to be shod. Although basically a farmer, Daniel still kept a forge from his blacksmithing days.

Jeb kept the billows pumping and the fire hot while Bart held a horse. Daniel measured, shaped, and put shoes on ten horses. Once the job was completed, Jeb and Bart only needed to pack supplies and hit the road.

Daniel told Bart not to worry. He would look in on Toby, Sparrow, and Hoot. "It's too hot to do much but sit under a shade tree."

"Those two boys can find trouble in the shade," Bart said. "I thank you kindly. We'll be back late fall."

They planned to follow the Chisholm Trail out of Texas, cross the Red River, and then branch northeast toward Fort Sill.

"We should make the trip in two or three weeks," Jeb said. "Unless we need to slow down for the women and little Sam."

The big man chuckled. "I rescued Katie from the Comanche on the plains of the Territory. We rode through some godawful country and a terrible storm. Crossed rivers and ran into outlaws. She never complained. Matter of fact, she saved my life. You needn't worry about Katie. As for Nancy, she's just as tough. When I first saw her, she was crawling around buck-naked in a prairie dog town screaming and digging. About fifteen braves sat their horses watching her. I figured I'd have to shoot her to keep them from taking her, but they finally decided she was crazy and rode away. I happened by her cabin the next morning and wound up staying a few days to help, since her husband wasn't around. He showed up after I left and forced her and Toby to go with him and his outlaw buddies. She managed to get away from them. I could go on for quite a spell about her. Sam's little, but he's tough as a hickory nut and can ride all day. He'll sleep in the saddle, if needs be."

"Sounds like I might be the one who holds us up," Jeb said. "I would like to go by way of Fort Sill, if that's okay with you. I have a friend there to check on. Or at least I think she's there."

"That's fine with me. Is this lady special?"

"Don't know her very well, but sure would like to know her better. She's had a bit of bad luck and may need a helping hand."

"I'm sure a stop at the fort will be welcomed."

* * * * *

CHAPTER 32

SPIRITS were high, as the little group prepared to leave.

Jeb noticed that only Nancy seemed reluctant, as she hugged Toby, Sparrow, and Hoot.

"Let's get going," Sam said, livening up things as he headed out in the wrong direction.

"Whoa there, partner," Jeb said. "Turn that bronc around. See the big cottonwood? Head for it."

Bart laughed. "I hope you're not giving him the idea he's in charge."

Jeb rode up beside Sam, and together they started down the path.

Plans were to reach the Chisholm Trail and follow it to the Red River. One thing for sure, the trail wouldn't be hard to find. Thousands of hooves marked the way from Texas to Kansas and at times all the way to Montana. The drives started in early April when green grass began to show. This late in the summer, it was doubtful they would see a cattle drive. The hot sun had baked the green out of the grass and steamed water from the rivers. It would be risky to make the trip this time of year.

Midmorning brought a bright sun, uncomfortable heat, and annoying insects. The tiny critters bit horses and humans indiscriminately and at every opportunity. The first creek they came to was dry, so Jeb pushed on hoping the next one would hold enough water for the horses. Each rider carried a full canteen, but used it sparingly.

Jeb called a halt when he found a shrinking pool of water in an otherwise dry creek bed. Riders allowed their mounts to drink, and then rode to a grassy area and dismounted.

"Loosen your cinch some, so Rascal can relax," Nancy called to Sam.

Sam scurried to do as told and made a show of checking the pony's hooves. He stayed active exploring the area, while the others prepared a quick meal and stretched their legs.

"I think I'm going to be saddle sore," Nancy said to Bart, when she handed him a couple of cold biscuits filled with bacon.

"Probably. You haven't been on a horse in a while. Not too late to turn back."

"No, I'm going. It's nice to be out in a different type of country."

Because of the heat, they stopped and rested often, even though Jeb was anxious to get back to Russ and Tulip. He missed them both, but was right in leaving Tulip behind. Russ would take good care of her. She was getting old and needed an easier life. That might apply to him, as well.

The novelty of the trip soon wore off, and the riders simply made it from one day to the next. The scenery was more bleak than beautiful, because the hot sun baked everything. Once in a while the wind blew, but instead of relief it brought hot air.

Jeb stuck to the well-traveled trail and, so far, had seen no one. He decided to cross the Red River at a popular place where a ferry was available in the spring, winter, and fall. This time of year there probably wasn't enough water to paddle a canoe. The biggest danger now was quicksand. As sunlight faded, he planned to camp on the west bank for the night and cross the next morning.

"Crossing the Red means going into Indian Territory, don't it?" Katie asked Jeb.

"Yes, but they don't roam as much as they used to. Soldiers back from the Civil War are chasing them onto reservations. Hunters are being paid to kill off the buffalo. You were with them for a while, so you know how important the big animals are to them. Poor Indians don't have much of a chance."

"They were good to me, but I sure am glad Mister Bart found me. I still don't understand why they killed Ma and Pa."

"The Indian live different and believe different from us," Jeb added. "White people are a threat, so they kill them. Don't make no matter if they're good or bad people."

Crossing the river was easy and the River Trading Post came into view. Several horses stood hipshot at the hitching rail, and a couple of men lazed on the sagging porch.

"Stay on your horses." Jeb stepped off Brownie and handed Bart his bridle reins. "I'll try to get some word on what's happening around here."

"Wait!" Sam hollered. "I'll go with you!"

"No, Sam," Bart said. "Stay here and help me watch Brownie."

Jeb slipped the thong from his pistol, as he climbed the rickety steps and entered the front door. He blinked his eyes a couple of times to adjust to the darkness of the room.

Two men sat at a table in the corner, sharing a bottle of whiskey. Another man stood behind the bar. There was a door leading to the back of the building, probably living quarters and a kitchen. The walls were lined with shelves containing a variety of merchandise.

Jeb approached the bar.

"Get that grub out here!" one of the men hollered. "You ain't at it quick, I'll make you wish you was."

A woman came hurrying from the back.

"Lillian!" Jeb exclaimed.

The man grabbed her by the arm and tried to pull her onto his lap.

"Let her go," Jeb ordered.

"I ain't finished with her," the dirty varmint remarked. "If you're nice, you can have a turn."

In two strides Jeb reached the table and upended it. Pulling his pistol, he brought it down on the arm that held Lillian and then removed her from the man's lap.

"Get outside quick!" he ordered.

As Lillian rushed for the door, a man grabbed her and pushed her to the floor.

"Where do you think you're going?" the man asked. He looked up just as Jeb swung. A fist hit him in the face, causing blood to fly.

The lollygaggers recovered from their shock and began to advance toward the ranger. Out of the corner of his eye, Jeb saw Lillian slip toward the door. To help her escape, Jeb shot one of the men in the foot and then ducked behind the overturned table. A bullet just missed him and sent splinters of wood flying.

"Drop 'em," a voice said, and all action ceased. "I'm holding a double barrel shotgun and will use it."

Guns clattered to the floor.

"Come on, Jeb. I don't think we're welcome here." Bart pointed the shotgun at the others. "You gentlemen remove your gun belts. Be mighty careful. I'd hate to mistake your intentions."

Jeb and Bart gathered the guns, backed out the door, and then tossed the weapons into a water trough.

Lillian rushed to meet them and fell into Jeb's arms. "Thank you for saving me again. Can I go wherever you're going?"

"Better get her mounted," Bart said. "We need to get away from here."

"My horse is in the barn. I'll go get him."

"No, you stay here," Jeb said to her. "I'll get your horse. Is there anything else you need?"

"All I have is on my back. I'll explain later."

One the of men in the bar stuck his head outside. "Preston will get you for this!"

"Tell him a Texas Ranger looks forward to meeting him," Jeb replied.

"This ain't Texas," one of the men called.

"Then I'll shoot him and drag his body across the river."

Jeb rode to the barn and returned leading Lillian's saddled horse. Once she was mounted, Bart untied the men's horses from the hitching rail and sent them down the trail.

"We'll make introductions later," Jeb said, as he loped out of the yard. "Let's ride."

* * *

THEY rode several miles at a fast pace.

Jeb pulled up under a big pecan tree and waited for the others to gather. He dismounted and loosened the girth on Brownie. "We'll rest for a bit and give the horses a break. Just don't get too comfortable."

"I'm going to scout around for water," Bart said. "Katie, shinney up that tree and keep an eye out for dust or riders."

"Do you think they'll follow us?" Nancy asked Lillian.

"Yes. The man who owned the River Trading Post came to Fort Sill and offered to take me to Fort Worth. Then he said I had to work for him. I didn't know money changed hands with one of the men at the fort. He never intended to take me anywhere. Preston thinks he owns me."

"I'm Nancy Jamison. The tall black-haired, blued-eyed, handsome fella is my husband, Bart. The little critter on the pony is our son, Sam. The tree climber is our adopted daughter, Katie. We're headed to a place on the North Canadian River to get a little boy Jeb found."

"His name is Russell McQueery," Lillian said. "His folks were on the same wagon train I was, but the wagon master forced them to leave. I'm so glad Jeb found that sweet little boy."

"Dust coming our way!" Katie called.

* * * * *

CHAPTER 33

JEB led the group to a dry creek surrounded by trees and brush.

He dismounted and took his ground sheet from behind his saddle. He threw it over the pinto pony and secured it with a rope.

"Is the pony cold?" Sam asked.

"No, he's easy to see because of his coloring," Jeb explained. "I'll uncover him in a bit."

"Oh."

Good fortune was with them. Whoever or whatever was raising the dust turned and went another direction.

Once they had ridden up the creek bed, Jeb called a halt. "We'll take a break to eat a bite, rest the horses, and stretch our legs."

When they finished eating and were having a second cup of coffee, Lillian turned to Jeb. "Thank you for rescuing me. I was so distraught after Nathan was killed, I couldn't think straight. When Preston came along and promised to get me to Fort Worth, I jumped at the chance. I only wanted to get to a place where I might be able to take care of myself. Turned out he had no intention of taking me anywhere."

"We'll find a place for you," Jeb assured her. "Don't worry."

Sam, who had taken a shine to Lillian, sat on her lap. "You can go live with us, can't she Pa?"

"If she don't mind a pesky little boy," Bart said, ruffling Sam's hair.

Sam tugged at Lillian's sleeve. "What's pesky?"

"Well, in most cases it means a child who is bothersome. In this case, it means a wonderful little boy."

Nancy turned to Jeb. "My canteen is about empty. Do you think there's water up ahead?"

"I don't know. There should be some as near the Arbuckle Mountains. There's lots of natural springs, but the water don't taste good and smells like rotten eggs."

"How are you supposed to drink it if it tastes and smells bad?" Lillian asked.

"Hold your nose and take a gulp," Bart offered.

"Are we going to cross the mountains?" Katie asked.

Jeb doused the small fire with the remains in the coffee pot. "No, we're going around the base of them. These mountains are full of big rocks that stick up out of the ground with terrible sharp edges. We'll deal with enough of them the way we're going, so keep a sharp eye out."

Horses hooves were checked and cinches tightened. In a short time, the travelers were on the move.

By late afternoon they could see the mountains. Although not very tall, they were impressive. Short grass, scrub oaks, and cedars grew on what appeared to be solid rock. It was slow going.

"How'd you know to take this route?" Bart asked.

"Old buffalo hunter told me," Jeb replied. "But it cost a considerable amount of grub and coffee to get the information."

"Did you come this way on the trip down?"

"No, I came by Fort Sill. It's between these mountains and another range called the Wichitas, which are nothing like these."

"Bet it's pretty country," Bart said. "Much different from the place where I found Katie."

"Yep, that part of the country is fit only for the roaming Comanche, Apache, and Kiowas. Of course, they don't stay in one spot long enough to call it home. They follow the buffalo, and also raid settlements and escape without leaving a trace. Their women can have a teepee down and be on the move in minutes."

"You must have spent a lot of your time chasing Indians."

"No, rangers mostly patrolled the border. There were a few times we went after a raiding party. I was after Burris, because he committed crimes in Texas. That meant I could chase him all over the country. Same thing with the guys I was after, when I ran into you."

"So basically, you stay in Texas," Nancy said.

"Yes."

The water they came to didn't smell or taste bad, so they drank and filled their canteens. It was getting late in the day.

"Let's move away from here a bit and camp for the night," Jed said. "Is that agreeable with everyone?"

"It certainly is with me," Bart answered.

"We'll move out early in the morning and cross the South Canadian River tomorrow," Jeb said. "It's wide and shallow, but dangerous because of the quicksand."

"How wide?" Katie asked.

"About half a mile. Maybe a little less." Jeb rode into a small grove of pecan trees and dismounted. "It'll take a while to pick our way across."

The others followed suit and began to unsaddle and picket their horses where there was some grass.

Nancy and Lillian unpacked the skillet and coffee pot, while Sam and Katie gathered firewood. A meal of sliced bacon, beans, and biscuits was eaten without much appetite. The heat seemed determined to stay around for the night, and every bug in the country came to visit.

Shortly before sunrise, Jeb scouted around the edge of the trees and then walked back into camp. "We'd best be moving. From the looks of the clouds there's a summer storm brewing. Maybe it won't get here until after we cross the river."

By daylight the group was on their way and well aware that change was coming. The wind picked up, as the sky darkened. Cooler air was welcome, but dark clouds and lightning flashes in the distance were worrisome.

Large drops of rain began to pelt the horses and their riders. Then the sky seemed to open, and it started pouring.

"Let's pick up the pace," Jeb hollered above the howling wind. He took off in a lope, and the others followed suit.

Bart plucked Sam off Rascal and set him in the saddle with him. Usually, Sam would raise a fuss but this time he didn't say a word.

"We need to find shelter!" Bart shouted.

"I know," Jeb answered. "I'm looking."

Katie pointed toward the east. "I think there's a house or something over there."

* * *

KATIE had been right. A cabin stood on a small rise not far from them.

A loud clap of thunder shook the earth and continued to rumble. Lightning danced across the sky, seeking the ground. She hoped the cabin was strong enough to withstand the wind.

When they reached the cabin, Bart handed Sam to Nancy. "Get inside. I'll take care of the horses."

Lillian and Katie handed over their mounts to Jeb and followed Nancy inside the empty cabin. It offered a safe haven from the pouring rain, but shook with each clap of thunder and rattled from the strong wind.

ite with fear.

d him into her lap and held him close. "It will be okay. It's orm."

king miserable, Lillian found some dry wood near the ted a fire.

lled near it, hoping for warmth and to dry out a little.

"Will Rascal be okay?" Sam asked.

Nancy tightened her arms around him. "Your papa will take care of Rascal."

"Where are Jeb and Bart?" Katie asked.

"Seeing to the animals," Lillian assured her. "They'll be in soon."

Suddenly, large balls of hail pounded the roof.

Katie was sure they were going to punch right on through.

* * * * *

CHAPTER 34

LILLIAN jumped, as the door burst open.

Two men rushed into the cabin. One was tall and thin, the other medium height and chunky. Both were in need of a good scrubbing.

Nancy clutched Sam and moved back beside Lillian and Katie.

"Well, lookie here, Slim," the chunky one said with a chuckle. "Can you believe our good luck?"

"Lucky for us, Joe, maybe not so much for them."

"My pa will shoot you!" Sam hollered.

"Just where is your pa?" Slim asked.

"He's on his way," Nancy said.

"Joe, watch the door. If he walks in, shoot him." Slim moved toward the women. "I'd like to get better acquainted with the tall, pretty gal."

Waiting until the men were not watching her, Lillian picked up a hatchet laying on the hearth and hid it in the folds of her skirt.

"Which one you want, Joe?" Slim asked.

"I like 'em young. I'll take the blond."

"I guess that leaves me the other two."

Out of the corner of her eye Lillian saw Nancy slip a hand into her pocket where she kept a two-shot Derringer.

Joe took a step toward Katie.

Sam attacked him, swinging, kicking, and yelling. "Don't you touch my sister!"

The evil man swatted Sam like he was a fly, knocking the little boy to the floor. "Cut it out kid, or I'll wallop you good."

"Sam, go stand on the porch and wait for your pa," Nancy ordered.

"No!" Joe ordered. "Kid, get over in that corner and stay put, or I'll tie you hand and foot."

Sam looked at Nancy. When she nodded, he stomped to the corner, mumbling all the way.

Joe again started toward Katie. She scurried behind Nancy. When he shoved Nancy out of the way, she shot him.

"My god, Slim. She shot me in the leg. I'm going to break her neck."

When he grabbed for Nancy, Lillian swung the hatchet. He fell to the floor and didn't move.

Slim pulled back the hammer on his gun. "Okay, ladies. Fun's over. Drop your weapons and move over to the table."

Instead, Nancy darted one way, as Lillian and Katie scurried the other direction.

While Slim waved his gun, as if trying to decide who to shoot, Nancy shot him first.

"Well, I'll be damned," Slim muttered, as he fell to the floor.

The women were dragging Slim and Joe onto the porch, as Bart and Jeb raced toward the cabin.

Sam flew out to meet them. "Papa! Momma shoot a man! I kicked Joe, but he knocked me over. Then Lillian hit Joe with a hatchet."

"What in the world is going on?" Jeb asked.

"These two varmints busted in and threatened us," Nancy said. "So we changed their minds."

"Are they dead?" Bart asked, as he dismounted.

Lillian raised the hatchet. "If not, I can whack them again."

At that comment everyone laughed.

"We're horrible people," Nancy said. "How can we laugh when two men are dead?"

Bart walked to Nancy. "They were going to harm you, Katie, and Lillian, and not think a thing of it. You did the right thing, and I'm mighty proud of all of you."

"Papa, where's Rascal?" Sam asked.

Bart pointed to a nearby cottonwood tree. "He's waiting for you right over there."

The storm blew on through, but not before everyone was wet again.

"Let's bury these two and get away from this place," Jeb suggested.

Later in the day, they stopped to cook and attempt to dry their clothes. The fire felt good, because the north wind carried a chill with it.

"Wind will probably change tomorrow," Jeb said, "and we'll lose our cool breeze."

"It would be welcome right about now." Lillian threw another stick on the fire. "I can't seem to get warm."

"Here, take my jacket," Jeb offered. "I'm not cold."

Lillian sat beside Jeb, allowing him to slip his jacket around her and let his arm linger a while longer than necessary.

"Thank you," she whispered, moving closer to him.

"If my calculations are right," Jeb said, "we'll make the Washita about midmorning."

Nancy poured him another cup of coffee. "Is it a bad one to cross?"

"Not unless it rained a bunch up north and sent water our way. Not many rivers are bad this dry time of year. We shouldn't have any trouble."

"How many more rivers do we have to cross?" Lillian asked.

"The Canadian is pretty much the last one of any size. When we cross it, we'll be getting close to Fooswah and Russ."

* * *

JEB was anxious to get started the next morning.

They reached the Washita before noon and crossed it without any problems. The country was mostly rolling hills with creeks and trees. Once in a while they saw a dwelling and even stopped to chat with a farmer and his wife. The end of the trip was coming, and all were ready to get off their horses and stay in one place for a while. Only Sam seemed always eager to get on his pony and ride all day.

When they reached the Canadian, spirits rose even more. In a couple of days they should reach Fooswah's cabin.

"Jeb, what if Fooswah doesn't welcome us?" Bart asked. "Where can we stay if not with her?"

"I have a feeling she'll be thrilled to have us," Jeb answered. "If not, maybe at least the women can stay with her. We can camp nearby. Never occurred to me she might not want us around."

"What if she is my aunt? What happens then?"

"I guess you guys will just figure that out. One thing for sure is she's someone you can be proud of."

Near dusk they reached the trading post. Owen Hunter was beside himself when Jeb returned and told him Burris was dead. He offered beds and a meal for them.

Jeb bathed in the creek, shaved, and had Bart trim his hair. The women bathed in private in a number three washtub with hot water.

"I feel like a new woman," Lillian said afterward.

"Cowboys don't take baths," Sam told Owen.

Owen burst out laughing. "Complain to your mother."

Frowning, Sam headed for the tub.

* * * * *

Part VII

Thlopthlocco

CHAPTER 35

CHILLY north wind greeted Russ, as he left the cabin carrying the milk bucket. He shivered from the brisk breeze, but knew it would pass with the rising sun.

Tulip raced by, braying, jumping, and kicking. Russ rushed to the house and set the milk bucket on the porch.

"Something's wrong with Tulip," he told Fooswah.

The little burro ran down the path with Russ racing behind her. Fear clutched his heart, as Tulip ran toward two riders coming up the trail.

When Russ saw Jeb, he sat in the middle of the path and cried with joy and relief. His friend had come back!

Jeb stepped off Brownie. He embraced Russ with a brief hug and then held the youngster at arm's length. "You've grown a mite. How are you?"

"I'm mighty glad you're back," Russ said, wiping away a few tears.

Tulip wedged herself between them. They both petted and rubbed on her, until she brayed with happiness.

"I brought you something. Come see if you like him." Jeb headed back toward Owen and Brownie.

Russ followed and then skidded to a stop when he saw the pinto pony. "I dreamed about him. Can I ride him?"

"That's what I bought him for. Climb aboard."

Fooswah stood on the porch, holding Summer and watching them approach. She smiled when she saw Jeb, even bigger when she saw Russ riding the beautiful pony.

She gripped Jeb by the upper arm. "Hensci, stunko."

Jeb shot a questioning look at Russ.

"She said: 'Hello. How are you?'"

"I'm good now," Jeb replied. "Happy to see you're okay."

* * *

SUMMER was an unexpected surprise. She went to Jeb, when he held out his arms and seemed content to sit on his lap.

Jeb was there as Owen told Fooswah and Russ that a letter had been sent to John Anderson to tell him about the dead couple. If the man showed up, Summer might be taken from them. They were both horrified at the thought of giving up the precious little girl.

"I doubt he comes lookin'," Owen said.

Jeb was both excited to tell Fooswah about her nephew Bart, but also a bit apprehensive. He wasn't sure how she would react.

Owen saved him the trouble. "Fooswah, Jeb here thinks he's found your brother's son. He's come all the way from Texas to see you. Would you like to meet him and see if you think he's your kin?"

She looked puzzled, so Owen told her again in Creek.

Fooswah sat silent for a long time. "It's been many moons since I was taken from my white family. Perhaps too many, but I will meet this man."

"I'll go fetch him." Owen got up and mounted his horse. "Do you need anything from the post?"

Fooswah shook her head.

Russ and Jeb walked to the lean-to. "We need to build a bigger place for the horses. Won't take much to add on to this one."

"Are you going to stay?" Russ asked.

Jeb picked up the shovel. "For a spell maybe. We'll see what happens."

"What's Bart like? Does he have any kids?"

"He's a nice man. He has one stepson, an adopted daughter, and a son of his own named Sam. You'll meet Sam afterwhile. He's a character."

Russ couldn't get much work done for running to see if Owen and Bart had returned.

"Lookin' won't get 'em here," Jeb said, as he mucked out the stall.

"They're here!" Russ shouted, dropping his shovel. At Jeb's frown, he picked it up again and put it away.

Together he and Jeb walked to the cabin. Fooswah was nowhere to be seen. Russ went inside and found her sitting with the baby.

"Are you okay?" he asked.

She stood, handed Summer to Russ, and then walked to the porch. He rushed to follow her and was surprised to see several folks waiting. He recognized Lillian immediately.

"Hello, Russell," Lillian said. "It is so good to see you."

Russ turned to Jeb. "You didn't tell me Miss Vaughn was with you."

"Thought it would be a nice surprise."

"It is. I like her a lot. But how did she happen to be with you? Last time I saw her she was with the wagon train."

"Stacy was being bold with me, and I was uncomfortable around him," Lillian explained. "He kicked out George Washington Scott for defending me, kept his horse, and sent him away on foot. Jeb ran across George, brought him back to get his horse, and whipped Stacy to boot. When I found out he was going to Fort Sill, I asked to go with him. Thank goodness I did. The wagon train was hit by Indians right after we left."

Russ turned to Jeb. "You thrashed Stacy? He was mean as all get out."

"He was mostly talk," Jeb assured him.

Everyone laughed.

Jeb introduced Nancy, Katie, Sam, and Bart. Each shook hands with Fooswah and Russ. Then all stood in awkward silence.

Bart walked to Fooswah and handed her the picture of his father.

She looked at the picture and pressed it to her breast. Tears pooled in her eyes. In a whisper, she said something in Creek.

"She said brother," Owen explained to Bart.

"Yes, that's your brother, Brad. He talked about you all the time and never gave up looking for you. It broke his heart each time he came home alone. Finally, he didn't return. We don't know what happened to him."

Tears rolled down Fooswah's cheeks.

Bart wiped them away. "I'm so glad Jeb found you."

* * *

LILLIAN helped Nancy gather dirty clothes to wash, while Owen served as interpreter for Bart and Fooswah.

Katie played with Summer. Jeb and Tulip carried water to fill the washpot. Sam and Russ dashed about on their ponies. When they got too close and raised dust, Nancy threatened to make them stop riding.

"I believe those are two happy youngsters," Lillian commented.

"Yes, happy and wild," Nancy replied. "Sam scares me sometimes with his daring ways. He is so different from Toby at that age."

Lillian watched all that was happening around the small cabin. "I think Jeb cares a lot for Russ. He sure is good to him. Heaven knows he saved me a couple of times. He seems to be an honorable man."

"Bart thinks highly of him. He hopes Jeb will go into the horse raising business with him. I think Jeb cares for you, as much as he does for Russ."

"Do you really think so?' Lillian asked.

"Yes, but you'll probably have to make the first move. I doubt he's had much experience with women. He's been too busy chasing outlaws."

Lillian smiled at Nancy. "I might just do that. I like him a lot."

* * * * *

CHAPTER 36

HOURS passed. Jeb watched, as Fooswah and Bart talked.

Owen stepped outside. "Jeb, can I see you for a minute?"

Jeb joined Owen on the porch. "What do you need?"

"Can you watch the post, while Hoktee cooks lunch for the elderly folks?"

"I reckon," Jeb said, "but don't know much about running a store."

Lillian and Nancy walked up about that time.

"I can run a store," Lillian offered. "I'll go with him."

"Be happy to have you," Jeb said with a grin.

On the ride to the post, Jeb told Lillian about the locket he took from the Indian brave.

"I don't know what to say to Russ. How do you explain such a thing to a little boy? Will the locket be a comfort or make things worse?"

Lillian laid her hand on Jeb's arm. "In time it will be a treasure, but right now it will be painful. I'll go with you, if you'd like. I think you should give him the locket before Sam leaves. Maybe Sam will help keep his mind occupied."

"That's a great idea. I'll talk to him when we get back, but I think it would be best for me to tell him alone. Now I kinda wish I hadn't found the locket."

"I understand how you feel, but I think he will appreciate having a picture of his mother."

* * *

AFTER lunch, Bart headed to the garden.

Sam, Katie, and Russ played with Summer, while Nancy checked the plants.

Bart walked over to Nancy. "She remembered so much. No doubt about it. Fooswah is my Aunt Alice."

Nancy gave him a hug. "Oh, Bart, I'm so glad."

"But she's getting frail," Bart said. "Wish we could stay a few weeks ¬d help her get prepared for winter, but we'd better get home and prepare
    ᴇs."

"Well, maybe we can come back next spring and try raising horses in this country."

"You're willing to move and live here?" Bart asked.

"Yes, if that's what you want."

Bart picked her up and gave her a big hug. "I don't know how I got so lucky. You are one in a million."

Nancy laughed. "I believe I'm the lucky one."

"I don't know if they'll allow us to live here. I'll check with Owen about it. If possible, we'll give it a try."

"What about our place? Daniel and Susan can't take care of it and theirs, too."

"Maybe I can find someone willing to live there and raise a crop. We'll just have to wait and see the direction things go here."

When Jeb and Lillian returned from the post that afternoon, Bart and Nancy explained their plans to them.

Nancy turned to Lillian. "What do you think?"

"I'm an outsider," Lillian said. "I don't want to intrude."

"You're not an outsider," Nancy assured her.

"And no one considers you an intruder," Jeb added in a firm voice.

"Well, in that case," Lillian said, "I think it's a wonderful plan."

"Shall we talk to Fooswah before we visit with Owen?" Bart asked. "Maybe Russ can help us get across our plan."

They gathered on the porch and, with Russ interpreting, explained what they had in mind.

Bart watched Fooswah sit still for a long moment.

Finally, she nodded. "Yes."

* * *

THE next morning Jeb took Lillian, Bart, Nancy, and Fooswah to the trading post. Together, they explained the situation to Owen.

"I'll talk to the council," Owen said, "but the tribe is touchy about whites moving into their land. One thing in your favor is they love horses, especially good horses. And where will you live? You can't all stay with Fooswah."

"Is there an empty house or cabin we could rent?" Bart asked.

"My old house is empty," Fooswah offered in a mix of Creek and broken English. "The one I lived in with my family. Until you return, Jeb and Russ can live there. I welcome Lillian to stay with me, until she finds a place."

"Where is your old house?" Jeb asked.

"East of my cabin about two miles."

"Good. It isn't far from you."

"I'm willing to lease land," Bart offered, "if that's possible."

"It just might work," Owen said with a nod. "I'll call a council meeting and let you know. They will probably want to meet all of you and ask a million questions."

"Are there any jobs to be had around here?" Lillian asked.

"You bet!" Owen said with gusto. "I need a clerk who speaks English at the post. You interested?"

"Oh, I'd love it," Lillian replied.

"What about you, Jeb?" Owen asked. "Do you plan to work or live off the land?"

Jeb reached in his pocket and pulled out a badge. He was no longer a Texas Ranger. His new badge said U.S. Marshall.

"When did this happen?" Lillian asked.

"I applied before we left Texas and had them reply here. This means I can live here and chase outlaws in the Territory."

Everybody cheered, Russ loudest of all.

Tulip brayed and gave Jeb a head bump.

* * *

FOUR days later Bart Jamison went with Owen to meet the tribal council. With Owen interpreting, Bart explained his plans.

The council listened attentively, and then asked many questions. It was evident that some of the members were not in favor of letting Bart and his family move onto their land. After several hours, no decision was made.

Dejected, Bart left the meeting, fearing his plan had failed.

"Don't get discouraged just yet," Owen said. "Things could go in your favor. Ride that stallion around the area. Let them see what kind of horses you raise. Might even bring that mare of Nancy's."

"Okay. Gather them up in the morning. I'll bring Ace and show them some of his tricks. It worked with the Comanches."

Bart groomed Ace and the mare until they sparkled.

When he and Nancy rode to the trading post the next morning, the area was filled with people.

He dismounted, threw his hat into the crowd, and spoke to the big horse. Ace immediately went and retrieved the hat. This received many *oohs* and *ahhs*.

After removing the saddle, Bart asked for a volunteer. A young brave stepped up and sprang onto Ace's back. On command, Ace laid down.

The crowd cheered and laughed.

Bart gave a shrill whistle. The horse came to his feet and began to spin in a tight circle. With another whistle he reversed direction. The brave didn't quite make the turn and flew through the air. Another brave stepped up and mounted.

At Bart's command, Ace stood on his hind legs and hopped around, causing his rider to slide off his rump.

The audience was loving the show, so Bart picked up a little girl and put her on the stallion's back. "Ace, walk carefully," he commanded.

The big horse poked along, and the child laughed.

That's all it took to win favor with the tribe. The council met the next day and granted permission for Bart and his family to move there.

He could lease, but could not own any tribal land.

A few days later, Bart, Nancy, Katie, and Sam were loaded and ready to head home. It was early fall, and the weather was already becoming unpredictable.

Jeb, Russ, Fooswah, and Lillian holding Summer stood before the cabin, all having said their goodbyes.

"We need to leave before the weather turns cold," Bart said, as Ace danced in a cool breeze. "If all goes well, we'll be back in the spring with everything. Including horses and cattle."

"We'll be here," Jeb said with a wave.

Tulip trailed along, until she realized Jeb wasn't going. As Bart laughed, she brayed farewell and raced back to stand between Russ and Jeb.

* * *

JEB made sure Lillian and Summer were made comfortable in Fooswah's cabin. Then he turned to Russ.

"Let's go see what needs to be done to that old house to get it ready for Bart's family."

"It's not too bad," Russ said. "Me and Osekee were in there the other day."

They saddled up and, with Tulip following, made the short ride down a narrow trail.

When they reached the house, Jeb dismounted and tied Brownie to the hitching rail in front of the porch. Russ did the same with his pony.

Jeb sat at the top of the porch steps. "Russ, there's something I need to talk to you about."

"Okay."

"Sit here beside me." Jeb reached into his pocket and pulled out the locket. "Do you remember this?"

"Yes, my mother wore it all the time. Where'd you get it?"

"I took it from a Comanche brave who jumped me. I thought you'd like to have it."

Russ took the locket and opened it. As he stared at the picture inside, his young body began to shake. Then great sobs erupted. Jeb reached for him, but Russ shook his head and ran into the woods.

No knowing what else to do, Jeb stayed on the porch and hoped Russ would not stray too far.

The sun was almost gone when Russ returned. His eyes were swollen from crying and his knuckles skinned from beating on something. "Thank you for getting this for me. My mother was beautiful and kind. I miss her every day. Now I can look at this picture and never forget her face."

Jeb reached for him and pulled him close. "Guess you're stuck with me and Tulip."

At the mention of her name, Tulip came to check on her friend. Russ wrapped his arms around her neck and gave her a big hug.

"And Lillian," Russ added. "Don't forget Lillian."

"I ain't likely to forget her. She's a fine woman."

"You should marry her," Russ suggested.

"Think she'll have me?"

"Yep."

* * * * *

CHAPTER 37
Epilogue

JEB smiled as he watched Tulip sit under a tree next to Fooswah.

A year had passed, since he had quit the Rangers. A lot had happened since then.

Lillian and Jeb had been married on Christmas Day. With help from Owen and others, they added to Fooswah's cabin to be close to her. Lillian continued to work at the post as a clerk. She taught school when business was slow, and the community asked that she be hired part-time until Owen could find another clerk. Then she would teach full-time.

Jeb's job as a U.S. Marshall demanded a lot of travel. He finally asked Owen about becoming a member of the Light Horse, which was the tribal police. Owen talked to the council, and they agreed to hire Jeb. After that, he seldom was gone longer than overnight.

Over the winter Jeb and Russ had worked hard to get Fooswah's old house was ready for the Jamisons.

As promised, Bart and his family had returned to Thlopthlocco in the spring, bringing with them fifty head of cattle and ten horses.

Russ had become a carefree boy, running and playing with his friends, and attending school with Lillian as his teacher. He named his pony Splash, because he looked like someone had tossed brown paint onto his white body. Occasionally, he took his mother's locket from its special place, shed a tear or two, and then put it away.

Fooswah enjoyed her new life of leisure. Jeb, Lillian, and Russ took care of her. She could sit on the porch all day or visit with friends. Although she didn't work hard, there were times when she struggled to make it through the day. Russ fussed over her constantly.

Summer was growing, walking, running, and talking. Her uncle, John Anderson, had come to see her. He was a recent widower, who felt she was better off with the folks who found her.

In October Lillian delivered a baby girl. In honor of Fooswah and Russ' mother, they named her Alice Jane.

Tulip was getting old. Her favorite pastimes were standing in the shade of the cottonwood tree, occasionally toting Summer around the yard, and eating bread. Russ groomed her each day, cleaned her hooves, and usually carried a bite of bread in his pocket.

Jeb thought of Ned Burris and secretly thanked him for leading him to all of these wonderful people.

THE END

* * * * *

About the Author

Judy Goodspeed graduated from East Central University in Ada, Oklahoma, and was a junior high school teacher and coach for thirty years. She has written articles for newspapers and national western magazines. Publications include children's picture books, western fiction, and non-fiction books.

Publications

CHILDREN'S BOOKS:
Emmitt Mouse Plays Santa
Perky Turkey Finds a Friend
Perky Turkey's 4th of July Adventure
Perky Turkey's Perfect Plan
Saddle Up

* * * * *

NON-FICTION:
Cowboy Sweethearts
Goodspeed Boys
Papoose City

* * * * *

WESTERN FICTION:
Jeb's Quest